Praise f...
THE ANNUAL MIGRATION OF CLOUDS

"*The Annual Migration of Clouds* is a riveting look at a dire future that doesn't feel too far away. Premee Mohamed has created an ominous world ravaged by climate change and a mysterious virus in a profoundly concise and captivating novel. The story expertly executes what all good dystopian fiction is meant to do: show us just how bad things could get if we don't correct our course in the present day. The climate crisis is real, and *The Annual Migration of Clouds* is must-read fiction for a glimpse into a potential future."

WAUBGESHIG RICE, bestselling author of *Moon of the Crusted Snow*

"A dark, strange tale of the future that elegantly balances existential horror against necessary hope. Premee Mohamed is astonishingly good, and if we're lucky, will be writing books for us for a good long time."

CHUCK WENDIG, *New York Times*–bestselling author

"To say a story is ripped from the headlines implies clumsiness. Premee's work is infinitely finer than that. This is a story of personal apocalypses and what they make when we all have them and of the gnawing realization that the world ending is the easy option. Identity and duty, horror and awe, all wielded with the expert hand of one of the best new talents there is."

ALASDAIR STUART, award-winning writer, podcaster, and critic

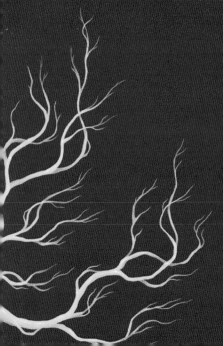

"A novella for people who want to see the post-apocalypse as more than simply bleak or hopeful. *The Annual Migration of Clouds* shows us how we can adapt, and hurt, and heal, all in one swoop."

JOHN WISWELL, Nebula Award–winning author

"Premee Mohamed's graceful storytelling transports us to a future that is both brilliantly imagined and utterly believable. I devoured this gorgeous gift of a novella, and it will stay with me."

KATE HEARTFIELD, award-winning author of *Armed in Her Fashion* and *Alice Payne Arrives*

"In gorgeous prose, Mohamed (*Beneath the Rising*) conjures a post–climate apocalypse future . . . Mohamed grounds her complex, chilling vision of the future in accessible human drama. It's an impressive feat of worldbuilding made stronger by the sensitive, nuanced characters and urgent questions about what people owe to each other. This packs a punch."

PUBLISHERS WEEKLY

THE
ANNUAL
MIGRATION
OF CLOUDS

PREMEE MOHAMED

THE ANNUAL MIGRATION OF CLOUDS

Published by ECW Press
665 Gerrard Street East
Toronto, Ontario, Canada M4M 1Y2
416-694-3348 / info@ecwpress.com

Editor for the Press: Jen R. Albert
Cover and interior illustrations: Veronica Park
Cover design: Jessica Albert

This is a work of fiction. Names, characters,
places, and incidents either are the
product of the author's imagination or
are used fictitiously, and any resemblance
to actual persons, living or dead, business
establishments, events, or locales is entirely
coincidental.

Library and Archives Canada Cataloguing
in Publication

Title: The annual migration of clouds /
Premee Mohamed.

Names: Mohamed, Premee, author.

Identifiers: Canadiana (print) 20210176326 |
Canadiana (ebook) 20210176539

ISBN 978-1-77041-593-5 (softcover)
ISBN 978-1-77305-708-8 (ePub)
ISBN 978-1-77305-709-5 (PDF)
ISBN 978-1-77305-710-1 (Kindle)

Classification: LCC PS8626.O44735 A76
2021 | DDC C813/.6—dc23

This book is funded in part by the Government of Canada. *Ce livre est financé en partie par le
gouvernement du Canada.* We acknowledge the support of the Canada Council for the Arts. *Nous
remercions le Conseil des arts du Canada de son soutien.* We acknowledge the support of the Ontario
Arts Council (OAC), an agency of the Government of Ontario, which last year funded 1,965
individual artists and 1,152 organizations in 197 communities across Ontario for a total of $51.9
million. We also acknowledge the support of the Government of Ontario through Ontario Creates.

PRINTED AND BOUND IN CANADA   PRINTING: MARQUIS   5 4 3 2 1

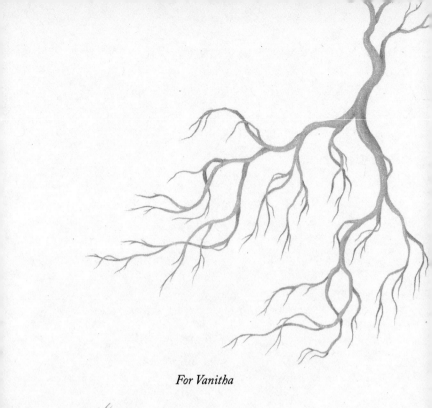

For Vanitha

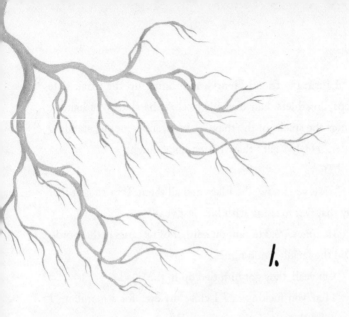

1.

You don't name it; you don't give it a name, either. They must have names they use for each other. I don't know what mine calls itself and if it told me, I would try to forget, I swear I would. It would not be like the secret names of dogs, which as a child I desperately wished to learn.

But the name on this envelope is mine, undeniably, printed crisp and black across the pristine paper trembling in my deathgrip. *Printed*, by a machine. Inside, the letter and the lump. Just like in the stories.

As if it is trying to read the words, the unnamed one visible beneath my thumbnail writhes in perfect traceries, tiny trees of green and blue. Graceful as branches in winter. The only pretty thing it makes, and even so I sometimes stain my nails with saskatoon skins so the patterns cannot be seen.

Which doesn't work. It ensures you can see it. Always.

"Reid!"

I turn; my friend Henryk is running up the black slate steps, breathless, hair over his face. As he skids to a halt, he brings the smells of the thaw — mud, snow mould, standing water. "Hey! What's that? Listen, they caught —"

"They?"

"*They*, you know. The Flags and all them. They caught that guy that was messing with kids last year!"

Messing with. He cannot, neither of us can, say the words. "Did they really catch him?"

"Oh yeah, they got him tied up in the quad."

"Hen, you fucking . . ." I close my eyes for a moment. "I *mean*, did they catch the right guy?"

"Oh that. I don't know. I suppose they must have." He pauses, and adds weakly, in the face of my silence, "They tied him up. I saw."

I look at my hands again, the whole landscape in miniature. White paper, black ink, green trees under my nails. The thing stilled for the moment: eavesdropping, too intent to squirm. "They gonna hang him?"

"Probably."

"Gross." I pause, because the answer doesn't matter, but I still have to ask. "Is he . . . does he have . . ."

"Cad? No."

"Fuck."

Henryk's eyes are large, loyal, a dirty no-colour, like sky. He says what he knows I cannot: "But sometimes I wish you *could* give it to people, you know? Some people. Who deserve it."

I know he doesn't mean me when he says *you*. That forestalls any hurt feelings.

At any rate we both know you can't. Cad doesn't move sideways. It appears spontaneously: and then implacably, silently, it moves down through genes and time like water seeking its lowest level. A heritable symbiont, they used to call it. Once and only once, I cried out to Henryk, *But it's not, it's a fucking parasite*, and the pain that shot through me was impossible to describe. As I imagined being struck by lightning would feel. Sight gone, sound gone, a roaring whiteness, transfixed throat to heels as if on a pole of molten metal hurled by a god. I never said it again.

This thing is of me, does not belong to me. Is its own thing. Speaks its own tongue. A semi-sapient fungus scribbling across my skin and the skin of my ancestors in crayon colours, turquoise, viridian, cerulean, pine. I imagine it listening now, keenly, sipping my happiness. Hatred twists my face before I can force it back down.

"Are you okay?" Henryk says, as if we had not just said aloud that the worst punishment for a child molester should be the transmission of my own disease. "Is it . . . do you think it's . . ."

"Getting worse? I don't think so."

"But you would know."

"Yeah. It makes sure you know." I don't want to think about it anymore. Quick, change the subject. Easy enough, given the morning's coup. "Look what I got."

"Holy shit. Holy *shit*. Is that — it *can't*!"

His shock is gratifying. I didn't think I'd get to tell him first, but I wanted to tell *someone*. I'm glad it was him, I realize. Everything he feels just pours from him like sunshine through a window, he cannot help it, he has no shadows in him.

"How is this even possible?!" He throws an arm awkwardly around my shoulder, startling me nearly off the step. "Reid! Oh my *God*. You got in! Look at you! You got in! Do you know what the *odds* are against that? Do you know —"

"Actually, they put it in the letter. See?" I unfold the crackling thing, *Dear Ms. Reid Graham, We have received your application to Howse University and are extremely pleased to confirm your acceptance*, and hand it to him. His fingers are black with dirt, but the paper seems to disregard it; nothing transfers.

Henryk's face is as red as mine feels. Blushing, squirming, they used to say "an embarrassment of riches," and only now, when no one is rich, do we know how it feels. I try to compare it to anything in my life, one single thing, and nothing happens; my memory is empty of such a sensation. My heart is going so fast I can hear it in my throat.

"The paper," he whispers.

"It's so *weird*."

"It's *so* weird."

The material is your first clue that we are out of our league. The only new paper we've ever seen has been grey, gritty, stiff, recycled a hundred times. From the accounts in books, themselves printed on ancient paper that still seems impossibly new, I know it can be made out of trees. But you don't dare make anything out of a tree now; they are too young and too few, and therefore too precious, to kill for something as frivolous as paper.

And this is not. It says (brightly, in tones of wonder) that it's spider silk generated by GMO bacteria, processed, purified. The entire sentence is an impossibility. This stuff, this pristine, even glowing white surface, is proof positive of a better world somewhere — carried a thousand klicks through who knows what, and still as clean as fresh snow.

And the best part: "Come here for a sec." We scuttle off the steps and plunge into the market, weaving through booths, stoves, banners, tents, blankets, shelves, till we find a low-ceilinged niche at the back. No windows of course, we're below ground level, but everyone has lamps going, and this will be more impressive in real dark. "Try to rip it."

"What? No. Absolutely not. It's your *acceptance letter*."

"Trust me."

"Trust *you*," he echoes. "Remember when you told me that that wasp nest on the corner of St. Joseph's was a —"

"That was *years* ago. Are you ever going to forgive me for that?"

"No. I'm gonna hate you for a thousand lifetimes."

We crowd into the corner, blocking the light with our bodies, and I tug on a corner of the letter as hard as I can.

It rips, but reluctantly — like gristle. Light flowers at the paper's edges for a split second, and then slowly, reproachfully, it knits itself back together, threads reaching for each other, grasping across the abyss. On my fingertips, it feels like the footsteps of ants. The light shines through my hands to paint tiny landscapes, red sky of skin and blood, black trees where the glow cannot go.

"Hooooooooly shit. It makes its own light!"

"Thou hast said 't, Caiaphas," I whisper back. "I got it just before sunrise, and it was just . . . I can't believe it. I can't believe it."

Act casual: lean on the wall. We try to get our bearings, stretch our minds till they can wrap around this, and still they cannot; I can't believe I had become so smallminded. Even the ink is a miracle, black and sharp. We write on our uneven grey paper in root dyes. Ours is a very low-contrast sort of world, requiring close study and getting fuzzier by the day. Little kids complain about the painful clarity of their scavenged schoolbooks: *The writing's too bright*, they say. *It hurts my eyes*. This, from nothing more than old paper, which does not carry its own light.

"How does it all work? Does the university send someone to come get you? I thought they never left the domes."

"I don't think they do. Otherwise they'd be out recruiting, wouldn't they? They sent a little tracker — sort of a, like a, well . . ."

"Can I see?"

I place it in his dirty palm: a nondescript silver sphere the size of a hazelnut, hung on a light cord of strange material. At its equator a tiny blue light pulses, obeying some instinct or directive that we cannot perceive. "You activate it when you're past the Zone marker, and then they come get you."

He hands it back, impressed. "So they can stay secret or whatever."

"I guess." *Secret or whatever*: I know what he means though. A secret not like our private strawberry patch, but like the hidden schools of wizardry in old books. Mystery, power, esoteric knowledge, and all the riches that must attend these things. Science tangible but no different from magic now, because we cannot replicate it, which we were taught is the point of science: *re*search, which is to say, you can find it again.

Instead the acceptance says: What do you believe in? And the tracker says: Believe in me.

It says one more thing, which is We, in turn, believe in you. Because they are trusting me to get to the Zone on my own, and in a little under two weeks. Non-negotiable. Some people would say it is a demand. To me, it speaks of confidence in my abilities, in their choice.

My hands are shaking. Henryk laughs at this, not mocking but glad, awed, hanging absently on the sleeve of my jacket like he used to do when we were little. We stare out at the market as it gets going: stalls rolling up, tents coming down. Ordinary morning. Laughing. Kids zipping around like sparrows.

It's all so preposterous; when I opened the envelope this morning, I guffawed, absolutely reflexively and all alone, like a cough. In my disbelief I thought it was best that no one else know. It's a joke, it's a prank, a fairytale. That you should be Cinderella, nineteen years old, sweeping and dancing and singing to the birds in the crumbling remnants of a city and a planet brought to its knees, infected with the strangest disease ever seen, and one day a being made of light comes and waves a wand over your head: *Go to the ball. Here is your gown.*

"Your mom must have freaked out."

My heart crawls into my throat and stays there. "I didn't tell her yet."

"Oh my God! Seriously? I'll walk you up." He pauses before we get going, and adds, "It sucks that . . ."

I know. I know. In his silence, which might strike an outside listener as embarrassed or unsure, I hear what he means to say: What mars today is that the person who would have been proudest of this is not here. We are bereft of the beloved dead.

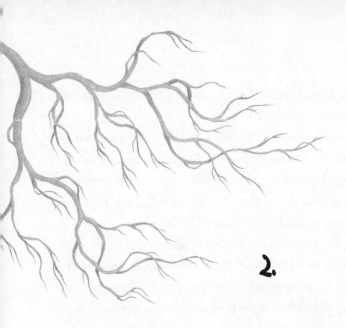

2.

We live in the Biological Sciences Centre; a strange affair, as I know from my reading, but what were people supposed to do? No one seemed to have accurately imagined, let alone zoned neighbourhoods for, a human existence in which no one in the world could survive unless it were close to a river in a sturdy building. And the university still had those when Grandma's generation was forced to find refuge, and so here we are today. It's not a disaster if you still have a roof, Mom always says. It's not a *tragedy*. Not if the wolf gets to the last piggy's house and finds he can't blow it down.

Long ago pillaged and sacked, our castle of brown brick and cream trim still stands, snooty, even snotty, above the ruins of newer buildings; ugly (really; over a hundred years old, and wonkily coyote-shaped on the map) but proud of its ugliness, filled with hundreds of offices and labs that slowly became occupied as the world shook itself apart. Home sweet home.

Mom and I are on the eleventh floor (Zoology), Henryk on the eighth (Genetics).

Grubby stairwells, concrete and brick, everything smeared with the passing touch of thousands of people, redolent of unwashed bodies and the outside dust that gets into everything. But redolent also of things that refuse to fade, of books, chemicals, specimens, ink, age. Dignity, maybe.

The persistence of the smell suggests that we are participating in, rather than merely witnessing the aftermath of, some proud and even noble long-unbroken chain of knowledge and study; but the truth is, of course, that the chain did break. And not once but again and again and again; and not just in the transmission of knowledge from the learned to the unlearned but also parent to child, elder to youth, country to country, every way you could think of. We live in the scattered links that remain.

Some of us try to piece them back together, of course. Impossible to resist at least trying. But the powers of the old world are required to reassemble it in full. Easier, though infuriating when you are surrounded by essentially intact existing links, to make a new one. Otherwise you end up as nothing more than an alchemist, screeching about theories based on texts even the ancients didn't write with a completely straight face. The wheel was practically the only thing that did not have to be reinvented.

Briefly, as usual, Henryk and I pause to catch our breath on the sixth-floor landing. The staircases are mostly left clear, concrete polished too smooth by too many feet to be really safe. Someone tumbles down a flight about once a week as it is without something to trip over. People brush absently against our backs in passing.

In silent agreement we squeeze into the window to study our valley. Unlovely in the early spring, crusted with a thin rime of muddy snow, the river still choked with ice, a single slate-dark thread of water at its centre. Sleeping tangle of grey saplings, dead shrubs of sepia or amber or faded dogwood red. Brown sparrows and dust-coloured pigeons. The only real colour is magpies, repeated shouts of iridescence, irritatingly clean in their black and white suits. Like photographs of actors or spies. How *do* they stay so clean in this crap, I always wonder.

Staring down at the trail of destruction from last month's storm, raw soil and even bedrock exposed by landslides, I can almost hear Henryk thinking, Do you remember when we — Yes, the dust storm when we were five years old, just when the grownups had thought those were all over, a relic of the past. Everyone rushed inside, not pausing to snatch up drying clothes or smoking fish; and Mrs. Chermak from the third floor, who had been sick for weeks and didn't look strong enough to pick up a fart, scooped us both under her arms and sprinted a hundred yards flat out, charging through the propped-open door ahead of a walloping cloud of dark grit.

A week later, when we had exhausted every drop of potable liquid (and several inadvisable nonpotable ones: a dozen of our neighbours were dead already of imbibing from unlabelled bottles and specimen jars), a scouting party went out for water. And Hen and I, and Tash and Arvin and Nadiya and McConaughey, formed our own investigative cabal and sneaked out as well. *Not far*, I said, so that we could run back. Arvin terrified, tears tracking down his dusty face, holding the door open, and Nads on lookout. But lookout for what? The air was still, opaque, a hot cloth stretched over the face, heavily unmoving. We pulled up our shirts, uncaring of exposed bellies, to protect our noses and mouths, and tiptoed into the dark orange light.

How had it hung like that, the darkened dust. Why wouldn't it fall? We stretched out our hands and stared as static tugged the filth to our skin, leaving a trail in the thick air the way it seemed you could do with clouds (so creamy, so solid) but the grownups assured us you could not. Stomachs churning with fear in the unnatural stillness. Like standing at the bottom of a grave, firelit, studded with the tiny corpses of sparrows.

I pulled free of Hen's grip on my jacket, scooped from a drift, cried out, the sound muffled in cloth like a chirp. The cupped handful of dust weightless to the skin. Like placing one's palm into nothing more than a puff of warm air.

It wasn't till it settled, covering the entire valley in a foot of black fluff, that we realized what it was: our precious topsoil for miles around, blown away, destroyed. We were so stunned we could not even have wept if we'd had the water to spare. And in the years to come . . . no, don't think about it.

Now I think: I could never do that today.

Or: I would never be permitted to do that today.

"Come on." I tug Henryk away from the window, and we keep climbing.

The door to the office and lab I share with my mother is propped open, labelled with our names under a half dozen crossed-out ones. Liquid noises inside, a faint lullaby hum.

"I'm going to go back to the shop," Henryk whispers. "See a crocodile, however, not until later."

"Indeed. Alligators are *frequently* observed."

He whisks down the stairs, turning at the final corner to wave again and make sure I wave back. The old crocodile/alligator thing never gets old. Best when there's someone older there to yell at us that we're doing it wrong, so we can do it even more wrong later.

I knock on the door, a perfunctory tap. "Mom?"

"Hi, baby. Just having a bath." I edge around the room dividers and clotheslines and find her in our living room, a metal bowl balanced in the lab sink over a lamp. My heart's going so hard it's like I can feel it crashing against the envelope in my jacket, a small kicking animal trapped there, scratching me. I try to think of when I've been so excited before and can't.

"Was that Henny? He didn't want to come in?"

"He had to go back to the shop." I reach into my jacket, touch the envelope, stop.

Mom is humming, scrubbing herself with a rag, dipping into the warm water, just like we do every week, but there's something different about it now, as if the letter

(as if my disease)

has slipped a lens over my eyes so that I can see

(as if the hyphae have gently adjusted something, hoping to help)

more clearly what I would be leaving behind: the body familiar not only because I have seen it all my life, and not only because it is shaped and proportioned just like mine, but beloved, because it belongs to her; and to the fucking *Cadastrulamyces* infection that roams across it like a river delta seen from space, huge twisting ropes of it, thrumming, braided, writhing under the skin and clearly bump-bump-bumping across every rib and vertebra.

This will be me one day: it gets more like this the longer out of dormancy it is, though in some people

(hosts)

it stays this way, squirming and dark; and in some it bulges out their limbs and backs and faces, knocks out teeth or eyes, eats ears, amputates fingers; and in some it brings paralyzing vertigo and narcolepsy, amnesia and dementia; and in some it just goes what we call in a truly hilarious understatement *off* and recedes till it cannot be seen except as a thin sky-blue tinge under corneas and fingernails while it overloads every nerve in the body and causes pain so nightmarishly terrible that the victims swiftly lose their voice from screaming. And you never know how it will go. You never know how the lottery will play out. The odds could not be calculated even when it was shiny and new and the world had not ended. Its intentions remain absolutely opaque, always.

You want to ask, What are you dooooooing in there, but you also live in terror of it answering.

I never speak to mine.

I wonder if my mother speaks to hers.

"Are you hungry?" she says, the age-old question, and I laugh and say no, the age-old answer, and then I fidget while she finishes, tips the grubby water into a pot of tomatoes, and gets dressed.

"I have big news. The biggest. The —"

"Oh my *God*, you're not going to tell me you're pregnant!"

All the blood has washed out of her face; I can't tell if she's delighted or horrified, but I'm too excited to care, and I plunge on, digging in my jacket for the envelope. "Mom. I didn't get knocked up. I got accepted to Howse University!"

"What?"

I wait for her to shriek, leap into my arms, but she's too stunned — like Henryk in those first few seconds — her mouth hanging open, poleaxed.

"Have to do everything myself." I laugh, and pull her into a hug. She laughs too, an uncertain squawk, and I let her go. She sways onto a stool, puts a hand to her forehead. Unlike Henryk, who turned crimson, Mom is ashen; the subdermal curlicues of fungus at forehead and chin stand out like soot.

"Don't faint!"

"I'm not going to faint, baby." But her voice is weak, and for a few horrible moments I can only think, This is it, I killed her, heart attack time, she's about to die of shock.

The moment passes. She rallies, pinkens, puts an elbow on the counter, even grins. "Well that's really amazing, isn't it? That's quite something."

"Yes! Oh man. I'm so excited I think I'm gonna explode. I told Hen first, I'm *so* sorry, but like — he found me on the steps and — look, when you try to rip it, maybe we'll have to go into the stairs so it's really dark, but —"

"All right, now calm down."

She's right, I'm tripping over my words, running out of air. I stand there still laughing, wondering if something's pouring off me that she can see, like Hen's sunshine. I give her the letter when she holds out her hand, and she unfolds it, reads it, strokes the paper, her eyes roving up and down the sheet, up and down and up again, as if she is looking for something beyond the words, like a hidden drawing or a secret acrostic.

"Try to tear it!" I say again.

"Just a minute." She looks up at me, dark eyes, greenish whites where the disease encroaches. "Well, I'm very proud of you, you know that."

There's a *but* coming. I take a deep breath, let it out slowly. There will be objections. Of course. It is understood that birds leave nests, but humans are not birds, and we all have to remember that. We can't fly, we can't hunt. We've all had the talk a hundred times, in slight variations, as if all parents have been given a clandestine copy of a script that has survived throughout the generations since we moved from the trees to the plains. In short, for years the world has only gotten worse: you can't just leave the nest like that.

And yet when it comes, it is not what I expect.

"But it says here you have to be at the marker in two weeks. No, thirteen days . . . Reid, I know you're excited, but let's just sit and think about this for a minute, hmm? Do you really think you're prepared for this? That you could get there in time and alone?"

"I . . ."

"And the thaw's started."

The thaw. The closest we have to the title of a prayer. And yes, I know that, I'm outside all the time, Henny smelled of it this morning, but I didn't stop to think about it. The thaw, when we dig out from the snow and examine what the winter has left us to work with for the coming year: where we can still plant or pasture, what greenhouses have been spared. Not one of us can be absent at this time of year. Mom didn't need to say that.

"Baby, I know we've all heard about places like this. The last remnants of the old world, isn't that what they're supposed to be? It was okay that they left everybody behind, because they needed to save what they had, to make sure they could help with recovery after everything that happened? And I know it's a, a, a very interesting idea, a really attractive idea. But . . . you don't really think this place is real, do you?"

I stare at her, unable for a moment to summon words. "Not *real*? Mom, we're talking about a school, not . . . not Santa Claus."

But even with the glowing device in my palm (returned to me quickly and efficiently as if I had handed her a burning ember), it's not enough. I'm torn between laughing and shouting; her cool nervousness is throwing me off.

"We can't even spare someone to go with you. And would it be any safer with two than with one? Anything could happen on the road. Come on, you've always done so well in school, I know you've got a good brain on you," she says gently. "Now, if you just step back, you'll find yourself thinking: slow down. Slow down and think."

I don't have *time* to slow down and think, there's two weeks left, there's . . . "Mom, they only accept a couple of students a year. From *anywhere*, not just here. Mrs. Cross has been telling us that for years. It really is less than a one-in-a-million chance."

"Well, I'm not going to stand in your way. If you decide you do want to leave us."

She smiles, but it doesn't reach her eyes. Behind her on the lab bench I notice an open metal box, a rag next to it, the enamel pins within a little captive flock of bright birds. Cleaning Grandma's collection. I wonder if I will be allowed to take one as a souvenir when I leave. I have my favourites: the unicorn, the black cat.

Best not to ask now. I know she's happy for me; she just needs a minute. I do too, I think.

I wonder if she said that to Dad when he left. If you decide. *If.* Because leaving is not what we do.

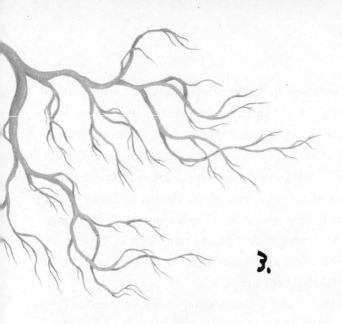

3.

There's so much to do today. Spring is coming. The world is swinging back around to sun, the most familiar thing in the whole world and yet it still manages to surprise us when the days begin to lengthen every year, like: Hello, me again, don't you remember my face? All our terraces and beds and rooftop gardens the same old things but new too, revealed in strange new shapes by the melting snow; and the strength-ening wind returning, carrying (we hope) clouds fat with rain. Maybe the same ones. How often have I looked at them and felt that strange déjà vu, the sensation that I have seen that exact shape and size and colour of cloud before, even though I know that's not possible? In spring, everything stays the same while it gets ready to change, but change it will. It is our most nerve-wracking time.

The sun is still a comfort. The sun, the clear air. I strip to my underwear and lie on my bed to soak it in, letter clutched to my stomach, the light making a tiny torch of each hair on my legs. All around us the sound of other bodies, other motions: clunk, thump, shuffle, snore. But in my office, it is just me and the sun, and the ants gleaming on the wall like a trickle of ink, shiny little polished backs. Clean and fussy as a magpie. It won't be like this at Howse. But I can't imagine what it would be like instead. I'm too scared to think straight. And yet as I think I got in, I got in, my stomach does a flip under the letter, the same motion each time, a dog doing a trick.

We so rarely say *sick*, we don't even say the name of the monster inside us. But when you get right down to it, how can I leave Mom, sick as she is? What if her Cad goes off? And how can I leave everyone else here? I have nothing to look to as an example, I have no one to model myself after, only those who have died and those who have abandoned us. Because it's not that people don't leave at all, it's that it's so rare as to be talked about for literal years, and each time, there was a sense (dim but persistent) of betrayal, grief. Maybe they did not leave behind a parent or a child or a partner, but they were leaving the rest of us. And we cannot spare anyone. First principles. So we rage and we mourn. Every time. Years in between.

In one sense, she has the entire community; but in every other sense, she only has me. For years I've been all she's ever had, and vice versa. Not one of those things you stop and think about till you're forced to. I can almost taste her fear in the air: for me, for herself. *Supposing something happens to you.*

I've never been outside city limits. What if something *does* happen? Alone out there, with my useless letter, the useless gadget.

And "even real," what the hell does *that* mean? Mrs. Cross has been doing the applications, the essays, the swabs, the forms for years. Decades. Why wouldn't they be real?

And what about the tracker? No one here has the ability to make anything like that. There are probably only a handful of people in the entire city who have seen artificial light. Hell, when I saw it, I stared for so long I thought I'd hurt my eyes. *Look at that. Magic.* Where did it come from, if not someplace that held onto everything that the rest of the world had lost?

Mom's right, though. I haven't said yes. It's still an *if*. It's not an acceptance till I turn the tracker on. Not really. To them, I haven't said yes. I haven't said no. When I am nearly at the front door, that will be when I accept.

Front door. Do domes even have a front door? I guess you could put it anywhere. But is that really where I want to go in the first place? When things began to fall apart, that's where rich people went. They said: *This is the only place you can live.* A strange thing to say, first off, because since we were kids the saying has been *A city is the only place you can live* (and you only need to look around you once to see that it's true).

But I guess proverbs evolve. Quick, too. Just like everything alive back then, between the droughts and the fires, the storms and the plagues and the thirst, they had to evolve in the space of just ten or twenty years, or perish. And in that space, the haves burned the last of the wet fuel as they raced to find sanctuaries they could fortify, secret spaces they walled off from the have-nots, to ride out the great disasters with their own kind, leaving us to fend for ourselves. Money poured into survival assets for the fast short fall, and then both money and assets were gone, drained away from everybody else forever, into a dry world with a few tiny shiny droplets on it in unmapped places. Like splashes of water tossed onto the dust, unabsorbed.

(Or so it's said. Or so it's said.)

I've never seen one of the domes. None of us has. None of our parents; none of our grandparents. Like the Cad, our ignorance has been passed down perfectly intact, maybe even gaining potency with each generation. Does that mean they're not real?

If they are real, are these people I want to go towards, in preference over my own people? The ones who abandoned us? Their descendants?

For several breaths (stomach revolving steadily, in great pain, a Catherine wheel) I picture myself very clearly: standing on a highway surrounded by mountains clothed in dead golden-red pines, the cold wind whistling through my hair, farther from home than I've ever been in my life, and no one coming to get me. Or worse: someone coming to *get me*. We've seen the aftermath of that. Blood-smeared kennels and shackles, withered placentas, teeth trickling like salt from lifted cages.

No. That won't happen. I will not let that happen. (Probably, my Cad will not *let* that happen. The medical literature says it wants to live. It wants me to do safe good things. They say it nudges you. Keeps the knife from your knuckles. Dodges you past the upturned nail on the sidewalk. Don't think about it, don't think about it, don'tdon'tdon'tdon't. Because if it does then what does that mean. What does it mean. *Just your body, right?* we ask hopefully. *Just your muscles? Just your nerves?* People go quiet and look away. I hate it. Hate. If it fucking *dares.* To. Even *once.* No. *Don't think about it,* I said.)

Maybe they have cured it, at this university. Maybe that is why in their application they ask for the cheek swab. Maybe they even privilege those applicants, maybe that adds something to your score.

My stomach flips again, brightly, hopefully, before I can squash that thought down. No, I'm sure they haven't cured it. They had decades to find a cure before everything began to fall apart, and even with all the immense powers and secrets of the old world, they never did. Everything was too late.

I rise, dress, comb my hair, tie it back. Rested long enough. *Nothing moves until you move,* Mom always says. The letter and tracker I stuff into the only secret place in my office, a tiny gap between two of the cinderblocks that form my bed, which I then re-cover with sheets and blanket. In truth I don't think the ants would be interested in either, or more accurately I don't think the ants would perceive either item as food, but you never really know what ants think.

The morning necessaries: dried clothes freed for good behaviour, folded, put away; flat spots dusted; rags washed and rehung; chamber pots emptied; compost rotated; vegetables monitored, trimmed, and given a long serious chat about self-esteem. Mom is embarrassed that I have never outgrown talking to our plants, but she also has to admit that I can coax more food out of the pots than anyone else in our wing. "Cause and effect," I always tell her.

"You're perverting the good name of science, Ree."

We walk down to the Dining Hall for breakfast, and then, as we had discussed yesterday (before everything changed, I tell myself, trying to recover my earlier excitement) we visit the allotment we share with our floor, Macyk Gardens, between Rutherford and Half-HUB. A few others are out already; we wave to Van and Larsen and stand on the far side of the fence.

It's too wet to seed — thigh-deep craters of meltwater glimmer in the last of the snow. Erosion on the west side: *Severe gullies*, I write on my slate. And we'll still see night frost for a couple of weeks at least. We've been planning all winter, just like everybody else. Colour-coded dots and crosses, triangles and squares, wiped off the tile, started over. What will fit here? What will fit over there? What needs light, what needs water, what needs supervision from rabbits or bugs? We do not say: *Unfit to be planted*. We say: *Needs extra work*. Then we build all the extra needs into our planting and harvesting schedule. There's never an empty . . .

. . . there's never an empty spot of soil. There's never an empty shelf in a greenhouse. And there's never anyone to spare. Not anyone who can lift so much as a teaspoon, a single canola seed. It's not just Mom I'd be leaving. It's . . .

Unmoving, still studying the water-pocked soil, I frantically count days in my head. Farrow, drain, test, lime or ash down. Pick rocks (even after so many harvests, we are still finding bits of concrete and asphalt and brick in the dirt). Compost. Sludge if needed. Test again. Stake. Label. Seed. Thin. Weed. Guard. Labour has been allocated down to the minute for months because what we support is a community that includes people who might be unable to work at any moment. Oh my God.

I just have to think. There's always a way around things, isn't there? It's not a wall. It's a fence. You can climb fences. I wish I could just sit down and think.

Mom says nothing, but it must be coming off me like sweat; blithely, we walk the foursquare of the field, chattering about seed swaps, which mystery envelopes we might win at the Farrowfair across the river next month, Greenhouse B repairs (nearly done), our chickens, Yasmina's miscarriage, Mr. Lakusta's novel. Think, think.

"Folks are saying this might be the year we go out'n the limits," says Larsen when we reach her side of the fence. I have no idea how old she is. Freckly brown skin eggshell-smooth under her thick, intricate hair. I like Larsen but more importantly I respect her ability, badger-like, of digging things up. She always has news no one else has.

"Yeah?"

"Opinions are divided," she admits, and jerks a thumb at our allotment — the decades of painstaking work to rebuild this soil from the scraped-clean stuff beneath the pavement. "They're still jawing about it. No one wants to say. Or no one wants to be the first. But there's seed, there's space, they say. Only the dirt and the sweat might be needed now."

"Where'd you hear that?" Mom says, casually. Always testing.

Larsen shrugs, watches her from under thick lashes. "Talked to the Dudas boys last night."

Such are sufficient credentials; they are our self-proclaimed local soil scientists, and these days, if you proclaim yourself anything, you must be able to back it up, or the entire city will quietly turn its back on you. *A lie is worse than a rust*, they say. Powdery-soft, stealing from leaf to leaf till the whole field is crumbling and rotten. We have to trust each other to survive. Trust each other to work, and to tell the truth.

"What about the Coy Scouts?" I say, trying not to sound too eager; I have other plans, after all. Though I used to dream of joining them, our fearless scavengers, freebooters, guards, travellers. The only people who regularly leave the city, go up and down the river. I think a few of them even have bikes, which is practically half of the appeal. You'd sell your *soul* for a bike. "Are they —"

"Taking people this year? Maybe." Her eyes are dark, sly. "But I heard you got you some good news keepin' you away from them hoodlums anyway. You ain't gonna dig in the dirt much longer, I hear."

"From *who*? I didn't tell *anybody*!"

She laughs, a few others drift over to us, the human instinct, herd instinct, flocking together to touch wings in the cold, still air. "People talk."

"It's only been a couple hours. What people? Henryk? I'll whup him with a rose cane."

"Congratulations!" Someone slaps me on the back, and I allow the excitement and pleasure to flush over me again as people repeat it, and yet there are those — I mark them — who meet the eyes of my mother. And with the same expression, too: not *We'll stop you* but *How could you.*

"She hasn't accepted," Mom says.

"I haven't made up my mind," I try to clarify.

"How could you resist? Sounds like fun," Larsen says. "No responsibilities. No work. Nobody to worry about."

"I'm not *going* to have *fun*! I mean . . . if I go."

She shrugs, which is almost more hurtful than if she'd said something. If I go, she will be one of those who never forgives me; and if I don't, she'll never forget that I wanted to. You don't understand, I want to shout. This doesn't just happen. This doesn't happen to anybody, and it happened to me. Doesn't that mean anything to you?

The silence stretches out till it's painful; I let Mom take my elbow and pull me free from the crowd.

"Not that way," says McKinnon as we wander west towards the quad. A big man, all shoulder and chest, as wide and flat as a door when he approaches face-on. A red scrap of cloth dangles from his jacket pocket. Here is someone who will kill, it says. But his voice is mild. "They're puttin' up a platform. A little bit of trouble this morning."

That's right: Henryk told me. I forgot already. Horrible. "Are they gonna hang him?" I ask, and Mom gasps.

"Well that's still bein' decided right now, Reid."

"Hang who?" Mom cries, horrified. "Just what is going on?"

McKinnon still seems sympathetic, but his face goes hard. Nobody really, no, nobody, he demurs. Just a drifter, floating up from the south, the desert places. No one here knows him, no one has claimed him. Kids missing last year. Some found, in various states of distress. Some not. Some in an unknowable limbo of no body and no return. And the man's confessed . . .

"What did he confess to?"

"Well, all sorts of nasty things, Mrs. Graham."

"Don't you patronize me, Charles. How did you get that confession? Who took it?"

"Mom, don't." I thread my arm through hers, try to drag her off; short as she is, she shakes me off and squares up to McKinnon, frowning up at him. He doesn't step back. Takes more than that to scare a Red Flag.

"You —"

"Stay out of the quad, Mrs. Graham," he says. "We'll let folks know when it's open again." His voice has not changed at all. We will be removed if we try to interfere. Maybe even if we just want to watch. People do, sometimes.

"Come *on*." This time she lets me pull her away, and we put our backs to the place where a platform is being put up. If their captive is not to be hanged then I don't want to know what they will do with him. And I hope I am too far away to hear the screams.

This too I would leave behind.

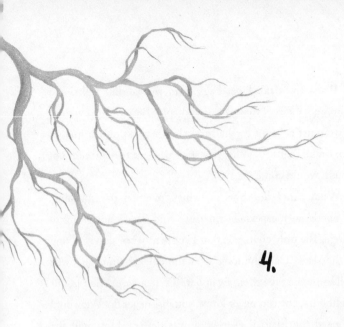

4.

Back home, Mom pointedly heads to her side of the lab and pulls the divider over. After a moment comes the soft, bristly hiss of spinning, a sound I have heard all my life, as familiar as a heartbeat and even less noticeable. I stand in the doorway and do snap calculations in my head about the coming spring. Good at math. Have to be quick about it before I lose my nerve.

Okay. Incoming, outgoing. Basic accounting. Quick.

Like most folks, we sign the majority of our annual harvest to the Dining Hall; on top of which, we keep hens (Sheffield, Edo, and Ratt) because we've got the room, everybody loves eggs, and you can eat or trade them. Our major income, though, is the plastic yarn, which gets those extras and necessities that must be bartered for particularly when you do not have food to trade. Few people have the know-how to make good yarn, and it's in constant demand.

That's the deal. I get bags from the landfill folks, and Mom and I shred, twist, heat, and spin. Between the two of us, we must account for half the clothing just on campus. If I go, I take that too. Whatever she managed to send out, not enough would come in.

What can I do? She's slowing down on the spinning, her hands hurt, especially when it's cold. That's not going to change. The only change is that I've spent years slowly taking up the slack. Can she look after the chickens on her own? Will someone take them from her? These are our friends, our neighbours, but you never know, you just never do. We would not need the Flags if everybody was perfect. How will she live? If I go, I'm removing more than myself as a daughter and a companion; I'm stealing her livelihood. And if her Cad goes wrong . . . if I . . . if . . .

I can't go.

It can't be *When I go*. No. *If* I go. If I leave her like this.

Think, think.

It is not freedom I crave. Both freedom and the desire for freedom are dangerous, as our long-deceased previous chickens Dewey and Tuckshop could have told you; sometimes you desire something you should not, and then you get eaten by a coyote. *Serves you right*, we said.

As a kid when I would whine for something, Mom would tell me, *Maybe you should want something else*. So freedom isn't the word; I am free here, I can do anything I want, any time I want; I would be less free, if anything, at the university, probably. It's a different thing that I crave. Similar but not the same.

A small bird crash-lands on the windowsill: sparrow or chickadee, barely bigger than a crabapple. They watch you because they like movement but they are also attracted by the glass reflections of the mirrortalk going back and forth across the river. Nads and Hen and I climbed up once to look at them; the polished discs on the three main towers were huge, though from here, they are no bigger than my thumbnail. They set them up years ago as the electricity started to fail, a clever solution for transmitting news and warnings when a runner couldn't make it across the bridges in time. Now I follow the stuttering stream of golden sparkles, absently, mind divided in half.

Endless chatter of predicted weather, wildfire status, random trivia, bird sightings, barter for various things (a trove of mason jars found in a cellar; two roosters; three buck rabbits in piebald, black, and white; sorted lots of books and bricks and compost and glass), everything interspersed with gossip, admonitions, proverbs, anxiety.

Like your mom, Hen said when we learned to read the flashes. *Worry, worry, worry. Do this, do that, do what you're told.*

Yeah, but you always do do what you're told.

But so do you. You're just cranky about it while you do it.

No I'm not.

Now I tell myself firmly, in my best teacher voice: I'm not abandoning her. It just looks like that. People will help her till I come back. Say that again, think it again, so it's real: Till I come back. I swear, I swear I will. I will learn what can be learned to help us, and I will bring it back.

Nobody's ever come back but *I* would come back.

I hold out my hands, surreptitiously, though no one is watching me, and hook my pinkies together. There. A swear. And it cannot be broken, except if one breaks the bone. You are witness, I tell the sparrow, if anyone asks. I look up again at the flashes: Bonus question! What was the capital city of Morocco?

Some trivia nerd on the mirrors today, anyway. I gather my allotment notes and slip next door to Yash and Maliah's office. Yash answers my knock: "Hellooooo?"

"What's the capital city of Morocco?"

"Casablanca. Did you come to ask that, little brat? Are you hungry?" She emerges from the back, untying her apron, and takes my face briskly in both hands to kiss my forehead.

"No. It's Rabat, actually. Everyone used to think it was Casablanca because that's the bigger city."

"And the movie, too."

"Go on, rub it in."

"Ach." She dismisses me with one of her complicated gestures, sending the paintings overhead fluttering. Yash and Maliah are the oldest people living on campus — maybe the oldest in the city, even the country, who knows — so they were among the last to see movies, the last to have electricity. *Imagine*, Yash sometimes says now, *wasting it on that! But we couldn't have known.* "Overrated. You seen the still pictures, you seen half the movie."

"But the singing scene. Where they sing to piss off the Nazis. And everybody is supposed to cry."

"We taught you that song in school, which you seem to have conveniently forgotten, and you did not shed even one tear. Pah! And they say *we* have memory problems."

"Who says that?" I say. "I'll slice 'em into ribbons and put 'em in the stew."

"No threats allowed. Ten minutes in time-out."

"Ten minutes! You tyrant. You Tiberius."

Laughter glistens behind her eyes, surrounded in rayed wrinkles so sharp they seem painted on against her bronze skin. Old joke. They used to teach grades one through six, so we could not, for years, avoid each other — I'd go to school, and there they'd be; and then after classes, chores with them at my side; and then home, all together, in lockstep, bitching at each other year after year. Now, mostly, they paint, and make paint, and gravely accept art from little kids, and sell or trade everybody's paintings in a kind of two-woman cultural marketplace.

It strikes me now, looking at them with the morning's changed eyes, that perhaps I am in the wrong place. Maliah spends most of her time in bed, though when she's awake she's as sharp as a tack. Lucky, that. Still strong. And no Cad. But even without it, how much can they do? It is not how strong they are or how much work they can do, but time, time. Time that cannot be generated, only stolen from one another. Time I cannot ask them to give my mother to make up for my absence.

Yash studies my face as I study hers. "What's the matter, brat? You didn't come over here to hassle us with trivia. And empty-handed, tch."

"Nothing's the matter! I just . . . today feels like it's been a hundred years long. You know? This morning, I got . . . I got an acceptance letter. From Howse University. And —"

"Oh, Ree! You're not joking? Unbelievable!" She sweeps me into her arms, and her shrieking brings Maliah sleepy and headscratching from her room, her thin face lightly baffled rather than worried. "My God, you vile little rodent, do you know the —"

"Odds? Henryk said the same thing."

"Henny is a bell that always plays the same note no matter where you hit him." She turns me loose with a kind of wrist-snap that sends me twirling onto a floor cushion. "He'll die without you here."

"Oh my *God*. No he won't. But while I'm here, Yash, I —"

"Congratulations, my darling. But how does such a thing happen?" Maliah asks softly; she leans down, yawns, scratches me affectionately behind both ears like a dog. "I had thought, because we hear nothing . . ."

"No one can run forever on their own kind," Yash says. "People need new blood. They've been recruiting students from cities for, oh — ten or fifteen years now. Isn't it, Reid?"

"Mrs. Cross didn't say."

"But she had you fill out the form —"

"Yeah. Form, essay, cheek swab. It was ten percent of our final grade. So some kids didn't bother. But I needed that ten percent something fierce."

"Because you fight with the bigger children, you climb trees, you don't study."

"Yash. I'm not six years old anymore."

"Bah. Lies. You got older, you didn't grow up. What did you write about, hmm?" Teacherly smile. She sits on a stool and looks down at me on my cushion, and for a moment I am six years old again, craning my neck at her as she speaks. The booming voice of wisdom, the hair already silvered, silvered for decades, the long graceful hands with their long nails painted with the skins of saskatoons. (Oh God. I won't be here for berries either . . .)

I take a deep breath. This is not exactly correct, but: "Reproductive rights."

"That's my girl. Pick a challenge."

We fall silent; their faces are kind, expectant, waiting for me to brag about it. Not sure I can. Part of me (I think now) did not truly believe Mrs. Cross would send the applications — that making them was just another ruse meant to buff some of the rough edges off our lives, manufacture a little hope, or at least distraction. A synthesized dream, when all the home-grown ones were tired and dusty.

And yet despite all the ways I tried to talk myself out of it, someone, somewhere, in a shiny and sanitized dome, read mine, and thought, Yes, we'll put her on the list.

How could that have happened?

What I had meant to say was not reproductive rights exactly, because it is very simple now, but the erosion of rights then that led to the now, clearly and neatly, like footprints in mud. They denied it all those years ago, but now, with decades of hindsight, we can see that there were no deviations from the path. What I had really meant to say was the depopulation of Earth.

First one then two then three, then a hundred countries at once, then two hundred, placed draconian abortion bans. Most had already eliminated sex ed from schools, and then (proudly, with parades) all types of contraception. Underground rings ran for a while, swiftly stamped out. Babies everywhere, you'd think, baby central, millions of babies, baby surplus. They began offering bonuses, tax breaks. But all those babies never showed up. Only the angry graphs and tables showing the projections, potential babies, quantum babies swirling like cherubs on a painted ceiling and nothing below it.

And then came this heritable symbiont out of (it seemed) Europe, out of (it seemed) nowhere really, something with no clear provenance, no signature, no stamp, no seal, that scribbled its name across the skin and kept you out of harm's way.

And people protested. They protested the bans and they protested the Cad and they mobbed anyone with tattoos of leaves or ferns or cephalopods. No one realized that the infection was cryptic, then dormant, then heritable from either parent. And so it spread, named and considered an epidemic at first — a flash in the pan, like Ebola or Zika or Covid, that would eventually burn out — and then, near the end, more or less endemic.

The only way to stop it would have been to stop having children. But no one knew that, to begin with. They thought it could be detected, fought, cured. And for many people, their own Cad did not manifest till they were quite a bit older and had had kids already, and those kids were themselves having kids. If you managed to get past the wonky sperm and the dodgy eggs and the pollution and the malnutrition, you still might have children that died screaming in front of you. Blaming you, as they died. And all you could do as a parent was give them to a doctor and walk away for the requisite amount of time that something brief and merciful could be done.

For generations we have waited for it to become normal. And it has not. We are still horrified. And there is nothing we can do about it. (I think: The reason it shows up late is that the Cad cannot bear to lose its host. But does it know that it's doing that? I didn't put that in my essay. Semi-sapient. *Semi*.)

And now, since we have rejected the laws of our ancestors: You can get an abortion. No problem. If you choose to do it yourself, no one will stop you. If you choose to get help, well, our "surgeons" will do their best. In the essay, I put surgeons in quotes because they're no longer required to hold qualifications — not like in Yash and Maliah's day.

Now, we have herbs, carefully cultivated in small batches on the roof of the hospital, that don't always do the job, and don't always leave a survivor. Now we have knives and hooks. Now, through broken windows we can hear and easily distinguish the sounds of an amputation, a surgery, an emptying womb, an interrogation; the utilitarian screams and moans of someone in labour can be differentiated with ease from someone whose Cad has gone off.

Mine is the first generation, I think, with these audiomantic abilities. Of which I am not proud.

I wonder what they would think about that in the domes.

Indeed, although I hadn't written about it, I had wondered whether the domes had rejected the old laws too. I hoped they had done better if they had. Nice and clean. Pills. Or safe, careful operations, with disinfectants, real antibiotics after. It was once assumed that if you had an abortion, or a baby, you would live.

"If I go, I'd have to go soon. I won't be able to help with the spring planting." I gesture with my clipboard, onto which I have carefully transcribed the morning's notes. "Or the spinning. Nothing I'm signed up for. I don't know if I would be able to come back for harvest, if there's a break, anything like that. If . . ."

"No *if*," Yash says firmly. "You're going. Of course you're going."

"But . . ."

"We'll cover your share. And we'll talk to the others. How dare you come over here and make me say that, to your face. What do you take us for?" She is indignant, looming; I can't tell if she's joking. Maliah watches us with wide eyes, her gaze flickering between us like mirrortalk. "No? You really wanted to ask?"

"I was trying to work my way up to it, but you didn't let me!"

"And I won't. Your mother didn't teach you a lick of manners, and neither, apparently —" she sighs "— did we. Listen. We are neighbours. We are family. We'll look after her if you go. Isn't that right, Mala?"

"Of course."

"Even if she . . . if her Cad . . ."

"How dare you. Get back next door and stop shirking. Go talk to your mother. Tell her we're here, and it'll work out. We'll make it work. And here." She glances rapidly around the room, even though I know she knows every single piece of art in the place by name, date, and artist and could find any painting she liked with her eyes shut. Flick: and one is gone from its clip, too fast for me to see. "You take that with you when you go. For luck."

"Thanks, Yash."

"Thanks, nothing. We'll see you again."

"You'll probably see me later today."

"God forbid. You're poison even in small doses. Rabat, my ass."

I stand in the hallway for a moment between our two offices, feeling lighter on my feet, more awake, letting hope creep back into my blood. What's the painting? One of Yash's own: a magpie, dark and neat and clean, perched on a branch over a creamy swath of clouds. I'll have to find a way to pack it flat. She didn't need to give me that. I suppose she'll just paint a new one if she misses it, and its absence will help her miss me less, knowing that we are together. That's how it works. They never had kids. I wonder if they wanted them.

I stash it with my letter and tracker, and murmur vague threats to the ants, and sit down with Mom to spin for a bit.

"I talked to Yash and Mal."

"Mm?"

"They said they'll cover for me if I go. And help with the spinning. I mean, until I get back. Because I know that was what you were worrying about."

Mom's hands don't falter, her face doesn't change, but the temperature in the room drops ten degrees. "Reid, sometimes I . . . really don't know what to do with you."

"What?"

"I can't believe you were . . . I can't believe you were so inconsiderate. That you went to two old women to guilt them into doing your work for you, while you scheme to abandon them, and us, for God only knows what."

Her voice is a hiss. My stomach churns, flipflops, has a colour: green-yellow and thick, like the slop on the river.

"God knows what," I repeat.

"Well, we've never had any proof that it really exists. Have we? Or any of the domes. Any of them. Now Howse alone has been sending requests for applications for just a few years. And yet, they claim to be a real university. Now people can make all sorts of claims. It could be a scam. It could be something terrible, run by dishonest people."

"Yes, but —"

"Whoever heard of anyone being 'accepted,' anyway? I haven't."

"People have been accepted," I say over my ringing ears. "Not here. But in Calgary. They sent word up. Two people."

"Years ago. Did they ever come back? Did they send word that they were all right? There's still . . . there's still a lot of people out there who might have motivations that . . . well."

"Mom."

"I'm just saying —"

"*Mom.*"

"— that it's quite a coincidence, isn't it, that *they* sent this letter to a young woman?"

We both fall silent. Because well, yes, a few years ago a group of people travelled up the Two from Red Deer and started what they called a "mission" in one of the churches across the river . . .

She shakes her head. "I didn't think you were like this. So gullible. You were always so responsible. Working to help the community thrive and be safe. And it wasn't like we made so many demands on you, specifically. Was it?"

"Mom —"

"But everyone has their duties. And you're handing yours off to a pair of — of ninety-year-olds. Don't you think they've got enough on their plate? Hmm? Or were you thinking about that before you went over and coerced them into covering for you? How could they say no?"

It's not river-slop that curdles in my gut; it's tears. Of course it is. Haven't cried for a while. Forgot what it was like. I want to stand up, yell, defend myself, defend my dream, my stupid dream that's just a couple of hours old, no older than the day itself, that she says is a fraud, a scam, a scheme, but I can't come up with anything, because she's right. I had sought out only familiar faces, never thinking of my burden adding to theirs.

You thoughtless, selfish little shit, I tell myself, and the words are swallowed as easily as chips of ice, melting as they go down. The way of all true things.

"I'll sort it out later," Mom says quietly. I wish she had yelled. "Reid, honestly. I thought we were past the age where I had to clean up your messes."

I swallow past the lump and watch my hands, the familiar motions. She says, "Don't apologize. You just want to make the world a better place. That's what they're preying on, those letter people. Don't be ashamed of *that*."

Around two, she bundles our finished skeins so I can take them down to the store. Something hard and heavy still sits where the lump of tears was, and I have to drag myself down the flights and flights and flights, out the side door, south, west. Steering well clear of quad still. It is quiet there, but that doesn't mean that something terrible is not happening, and I don't want to know.

That's not true. I do want to know. I don't want to watch, though. I want to look away and then have it be done, whatever it is.

Maybe that's the Cad. Or maybe I'm just getting older and more squeamish. Who knows?

(That without a name knows.)

(Yeah. That would be the only one who does know. And it won't tell me. Fucker.)

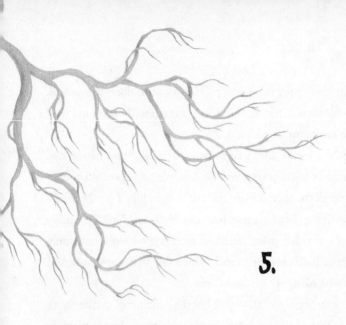

5.

The store is about as busy as usual, sunny, gusts of herbs and frying food covering the less savoury odours of compost and scavenged rubbish. A long time ago the university built this place for performances, and it never lets you forget it. The building itself puts on a show. Swoops and arches and the dance of untouched glass. Here where we haggle and cajole was where people would meet before the shows, and back there behind the locked doors is the stage, the encircling seats mouse-eaten and broken now, the curtains long gone like any piece of contiguous fabric large enough to be useful. Seen it all in photos. Always wonder what it was like, watching a show back then. The dresses and suits from the books. The hush, the stage lights.

Now I give the yarn to Bashir at the west counter and let him weigh it and put the credits into the book under *Graham, R. and C.*, and then I go over to the east counter and slide onto the empty stool next to Henryk, who doesn't even look up before whispering, "God, help me count these, would you? I'm losing my mind."

"It's hardly advanced calculus, Henryk," says Mrs. Cross tartly, as I scoop over half of her pile of paper and thumb through the sheets. Fifty, then fifty, then fifty. I tie them into bundles and enter them into the book and look up uncertainly into her pale, querulous face, topped with impossibly orange hair. Has she heard? Impossible that she hasn't. And yet, she hasn't congratulated me . . .

I open my mouth to give her the good news, maybe thank her for insisting we write those essays, then close it again, as if I can hear my mother's voice about to emerge instead of my own. We all turn into our mothers, that's the joke. But I am. And I will. I have no choice. And I won't even be there to see what she becomes.

Henryk says, "I'm . . . I'm still getting forty-nine here, Mrs. Cross."

"Are you suggesting that I am deliberately miscounting my product, *Mister* Mandrusiak?"

"No, ma'am —"

"Or that I am too old or . . . or decrepit to count it correctly?"

"No, ma'am!" His hands are shaking now, sweat bursting visibly from his fingertips. That'll only make it worse, and he knows it. Under the white-hot, face-destroying beam of her gaze, I grab the stack from him and slide it across the smooth plastic, minutely dented and scarred from the tiny but ceaseless impacts of decades of pens, books, fingernails, and tokens. Of course it's fifty sheets; two of them have gotten stuck together. I pry them gently apart with the edge of my thumb, tie, record. She double-checks the entries in the book, leaves with her face glowing.

"I thought she was going to mark me down," Henryk says gloomily.

"School's been over for a month. She can't give you marks anymore."

"I know. I'm still having nightmares. How come you didn't say anything about your letter?"

I shrug with difficulty; the weight inside me is still there, physical, smushing things down, pressing my ribs out. It has edges, this pain. Facets. I realize I am curling around it, my arms enclosing my torso, rumpling my too-big jacket like a bird puffing up in the cold. The sparrow, I think. The witness.

Henryk's expression is lightly reproachful. He says, "She's the whole reason you got in."

"Yeah." But I'm selfish, I want to tell him, I'm an ingrate, don't you know that, isn't it obvious? So obviously I can't thank her. I'm too busy shirking my work and abandoning my mother and my home. See, here, this mass inside me, black and dense as coal.

Through the cracked glass above us the light dims, returns, dims again. Clouds racing each other to get wherever they're going. Like they're such bigshots. In the greyness, I say, "I'll tell her later."

"What did your mom say? She must have freaked out."

" . . . Yes. I would definitely say that she did that. Yes."

"That's awesome!"

Someone I don't know comes to our counter with rabbit jerky; it smells nice, if maybe a little underdried, but it'll never have a chance to go bad. That's a treat you can't get in the Dining Hall, and it'll be purchased and eaten in minutes, probably before I leave. Henryk weighs it, puts it in the right cubbyhole, marks it down in the book, gives the boy his tokens.

I lower my voice, press down hard on the mass of tears. "No, Mom says it's a scam. A trick to get young women out to the middle of nowhere. No one's ever seen these places, she says."

"Well," Henryk says after a long, judicious breath, "no one's ever seen Paris, either."

"Yeah, but there's pictures."

"Could be faked."

"Movies."

"*We've* never seen movies of Paris."

He is complacent, unruffled. This is enough argument for him. He has faith in the letter and the necklace. Why shouldn't he? We are asked to take many, many things for granted. More than anyone who's ever lived before us. They could look something up in five minutes, or Zoom someone who lived far away. Even, for a little while, talk to the people on Mars. So they say. Arguably, we have less evidence that a mission went to Mars than we do that a single university in the mountains may exist. And which is more likely?

"Listen." He positions his forearms on the counter to soak up a weak ray of sunshine. "People in Paris know Paris is there. A city's the only place you can live now. So what if people *here* don't think there's a Paris? Or an Australia or Brazil or whatever. Who cares? If a thing is a thing, it's still a thing even if people don't think it's a thing."

"What?"

"You know what I mean."

" . . . Anyway, she also said I would miss planting. She's worried."

"Oh. Well that's true. You could ask around before you go. Or put something up on the board . . . or ask Larsen if someone's got spare capacity or whatever."

"There's no spare capacity. And I don't want to *beg*."

"I didn't say beg."

I don't want to tell him I didn't even want to get near Larsen, seeing her reaction this morning, but went to two old ladies next to my office on my same floor. Literally the least possible effort I could have made, just ahead of lying on the floor and waiting for someone to carry me to the dome. My eyes smart with tears.

"It'll get *done*," he says at my listless nod. "Reid! You don't think we'd just . . . ignore her once you were gone. Nobody's like that. Well, most people aren't like that."

"There's always a couple assholes."

"There's always a couple. But we'd protect her from whoever. You know that."

"Who needs protecting?"

A shadow looms, not a cloud one but a proper one, heralded by a tremendous waft of trapped smoke — Koda, who runs the east soapworks. Smell of ashes, old teardrops of chemical burns burned pale into her reddish-brown forearms. "Here ya go, babies. Get a whiff of that."

She plops six bars on the counter, neatly cut, resinous green, and turns to me interestedly as Henryk gets them in the system. "What now, brains? No one's on ya about the school letter, are they? I'd sort 'em out myself, but . . . " With theatrical nonchalance, she studies her gleaming nails, clean as a whistle. "Well. You got you enough practice in that particular area of expertise. What with this one around."

"Hey!" says Henryk.

"Nobody's getting into a scrap with anybody," I say, firmly. "God forbid. Little old for that, don't you think?"

"Never too old to remind people not to fight."

"By splattering them into the ground."

"Yep."

"It's nothing, anyway, Ko," I say all in a rush. "It's just, I'm worried about my mom, because it's the thaw —"

She snorts, a magnificent production in someone so big; her disdain is a five-act play. "What, you think you're so irreplaceable, you think the whole system falls apart less one person?"

"No! No, it's not that. It's just . . . Mom's not getting any younger, and —"

"Neither are you. You're gonna throw away this chance because everybody ages one day per day?"

"I mean, what if something happens to her while I'm gone? What if I can't come back? She'll be alone in there, how can I possibly —"

She shrugs. "There's no guarantees in life, kid. What if you stay put and we have another dust storm like when you was little? It ain't people runs the system. It's water."

"But the grids, the seeds, the schedules —"

"Sure, it's gonna suck trying to fill your spot. Larsen's gonna be pissed."

"She's already pissed. And I didn't even say I was going to go. And the *yarn* —"

"Let me finish. It's gonna suck, *but*," Koda says, raising a finger, "if we're gonna be stretched thin and pissed off at someone, this is the best reason. Reid, imagine what you'll learn, the folks you'll meet. Imagine what you could do! We can't give you anything like that here."

"I *know* that, but . . ."

"But you're gonna cry. Jesus." She leans closer; Henryk and I do too. The counter still smells sweetly of spruce soap, though it only held it for a moment. "What you want is something that don't exist anymore. Insurance. Now that's something we've tried a couple times, and it never works out. But what we could do is give her some savings. Just for her. Would that make you feel better? A little cache?"

"A little what?"

"Listen. I'm probably going to regret this. But I'm gonna offer anyway. To you, and only to you. I'm putting together a pig hunt in the valley. Friday. Hmm?"

My *God*. It's an invitation not quite on par with the university acceptance, but the startled lurch in my gut is no different. I've never been invited to one — never even heard rumours of one before it happened, in fact. Even the Coy Scouts don't hunt pigs. People have died.

But it's a lot of food, and game remains the one thing it's understood you aren't obliged to share, in a world where we share everything down to underpants and hairbrushes. If I went, and we got even a single pig, my portion, a tenth or a dozenth of that meat, would be tremendous. And it would be Mom's alone after I left.

Dried and smoked, Mom's share would set her up to barter for a long, long time. But most importantly, she would know what I meant by it. Meant to look after her even if I wasn't here: to prove incontrovertibly that I was thinking of her and not myself. Why risk death right before I had to leave for meat I would not even get a chance to eat? Why not just leave? Because of her, that's why.

This is a tremendous offer in too many respects to turn down: in reputation, mine and Koda's; in opportunity; in respect; in experience; in sheer calories. She would not have made such an offer out of pity for either me or my mother. She thinks I can do it. For a moment I love her with everything in me. "I'm in."

"Me too," Henryk says after a beat.

Koda hides her surprise at that, but a muscle near her mouth twitches. "All right. I'll send details."

"Thanks, Ko. I mean it."

She punches my shoulder in a friendly fashion, making my teeth click together. Neither of us needs to be told to keep it to ourselves. Too many people would try to stop us. To interfere, even sabotage. Or worse yet, invite themselves along. The secrecy is what works about a pig hunt, they say, because the things are skittish, and they have ways of knowing. I do not myself think, as some half-jokingly do, that the local magpies and crows are used as spies, but it is a fact that no one ever seems to know when one of the hunts is happening, and that is by design. We are all good actors when we need to be.

When she is gone, I punch Henryk too, not hard enough to hurt but as meaningful punctuation before I speak.

"Ow! You need a time-out!"

"What are you *doing*?"

"What do you mean?"

"You know damn well what I mean!" I glare at him till his face begins to waver. In this light his no-colour eyes seem even more watery and wan — shaking, then still. When I was diagnosed with Cad, he bawled in front of me, and my first reaction had been utter shock: as often as we had gotten hurt, as often as he had been beaten up and humiliated, and me too for merely associating with him, even as we had seen our closest friend dying of it, still I had never seen him cry. Even the next year, when his parents died, he had not cried. "I oughta throw you in the shitpond and hold you under. You're going to get yourself fucking killed!"

"Oh, and you're not? What makes *you* so special, huh?"

We narrow our eyes at each other, not quite joking. Or I'm not, anyway. He never would have agreed if he had been alone, I know. He would have laughed it off. Thanked her for the offer, maybe. Given her a dozen other names. Not mine. He only wanted in because I was there, and I was asked. It's scribbled all over his face.

Finally, he looks away. I do not remotely feel as if I have won, or that any of the questions I meant to ask him with my look have been answered, which I feel is deserved; *use your words, kids*, they used to tell us. After a minute I nudge him with my elbow, not exactly an apology. If we cannot agree on our motivation, we can at least agree on our inexperience.

"Listen, let's go look for rabbits tomorrow down in the valley."

He perks up visibly; even his hair seems to spring a little off his forehead. "Yeah! Like, a recon mission. Like spies."

"Bunny spies."

We briefly discuss logistics, where to meet, what to bring (unaccountably, we are both out of arrows; I have shafts, but no time to re-tip them), where to climb down. A silly mission; thirty or forty families on campus breed rabbits for fur and meat, and generations of jealous trading and competition have produced juicy refined multicoloured monsters as big as toddlers, so of course no one wants the skinny, gamey wild hares; even their thin pelts are worthless compared to our spoiled domestics. But we haven't hunted in months, and we have lost our old familiarity with the movement through brush and limb, mud and tree. We need that back.

I wonder what they farm at Howse. But a place that can make paper out of not even spider silk but designer bacteria counterfeiting the stuff must be doing things that we only read about from before the disasters. Not farms but cloned livestock in white-lit aerodromes. Or not even. Less messy than that. Vats, or lab meat, grown in neat lozenges. Clinical and clean. No one would farm if you could help it. Not real animals, with all the different ways they can sicken and die. They would think differently in the domes. (Oh God. Oh God, what will I do there, what if I fail, what if they realize city people are different, what if living here has broken my brain, what if —)

(No. They lived through all this too.)

(It's not the same!)

It was not instantaneous, the "end of the world," the way it is in nightmares. The sky didn't tear open around an asteroid, the earth didn't swallow us up. And of course, the world did not end at the same time for everyone. No one back then would have been able to say: This is the day our world ended. Or even: This is the year.

On a human scale it was slow enough that for a long time it did not seem truly dire; on a geological scale it seemed that nothing was happening; till suddenly the feedback cycles tipped over, became too front-heavy to regulate themselves. Nothing could be shipped or driven between cities, let alone countries. Parts could not be found or made to meet the maintenance needs of stopgaps: wind turbines, solar panels. And then the lights went out. Flickered feebly back on, as governments and billionaires threw money at the problems. But money was no more help than marches. You could not buy a new world into existence. And at last, the lights went out for good.

So here we are. The survivors of the darkest years, the descendants of those who spent decades clawing back into the light. Maybe the people who run the dome will look at me like I am some strange animal, some unevolved thing. I hope they will not.

On my way out of the store, back into the mud and the ice, someone else comes in and unwinds the scarf from his face to make sure I see his nod — Rene, distracted and haunted, the shadows under his eyes like ink. I pause to watch him cross to Bashir, watch them speak. Sun speeds after cloud, a stray stream of brightness unfortunately highlighting Bashir's slender arm as he rises and writes a name on the board behind the counter. I can't see from here, but it's under the longest and most populated column, in which the letters are barely an inch high — suicides. I don't recognize the name; they must live on the other side of campus. I give Henryk one last wave and go.

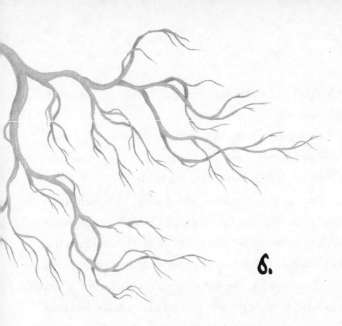

6.

Before sunrise I dress and slide quietly outside, blocking the side door with my foot at the last moment so it does not slam. The mist is so thick that I leave a clear wake behind me, swirling in sluggish spirals. Darkness, the pre-shine of dawn. A chickadee sings. Little survivor, they don't migrate; none of the migratory birds come back now. This one hunkered down over the winter. Hardcore. (What does that mean? The core of what? We get half our slang from water-swollen novels spanning decades. An endless puzzle, figuring them out.)

In the fog, I make out two familiar silhouettes about a second before I run into them; no way to hide, so I stop and say hello. Yash looks up from her slate and gives me a sneer of greeting. "What are you doing out here, eh? Up early to make trouble?" Before I can respond, she points imperiously at the bare square of ground at their feet, already marked with twine and stakes. "Look at this. My love, the great barbarian, the Visigoth, she wants to destroy the entire history of artistic achievement —"

"Oh, come on, Yash —"

"— and plant *flowers*!"

"Not on all of it! Just around the border!"

I pretend to be appalled, and I stand with them for a moment, studying their paint garden. Dead sticks of perennials, bare scoops of last year's annuals, filled with ice. In this they plant only things that can contribute to their paintings or, at the very least, dye, but there is no market for it, not really. And I suppose if I were nearing a century and had lived through the end of the world, I might like to say "fuck it" and plant some flowers too. Mal smiles at me as if she can hear what I'm thinking.

"Horrible," I tell Yash consolingly. "I hate it as an unfilled can."

"Exactly. Exactly, I tell her, art is all that separates us from the beasts of the field."

"Flowers are art," Mal protests.

"Art that dies."

"Everything dies."

Yash throws her hands up, nearly dropping her slate. While they bicker, I slink away, leaving only my trail in the fog.

Even this early, there are others out. The trick to moving unseen is not to skulk or hide behind things, but move fast, confidently, so that it seems that you have somewhere to be, and that somewhere will soon be out of the person's field of vision. I put my head up and throw my shoulders back, my scarf flapping behind me. It's a couple of degrees above freezing; the walkways have a thin slick of ice where they hold the night's cold separate from the air.

I don't know what I'm doing except that I stayed up too late last night wondering if I would hear what they were doing to the kidnapper — whose name I have never heard. Another unnamed. I move fast to the edge of quad, hiding behind one of the huge dead trees in case any of the Flags are still there. But no one is.

The platform is untenanted, somewhat tilted, as if hastily assembled. They keep it in Sub, I remember now. You don't see it very often, you forget what it looks like. Bring it out for speeches sometimes, warnings, announcements, whatever. And this. Things like this. I should not be here: but I want to know something that no one else knows. That Larsen does not know, that Henryk does not know. I want, maybe, to touch the cord they use and reuse, bright orange in the darkness.

But this was clearly not a hanging. The platform bears an enormous splattered stain, fresh, soaked deep into the wood. Not frozen — too salty to freeze at this temperature. A relief map: I know enough of blood to know that it piles up sometimes when it pools. When it is spilled, and then sets, and then more is spilled on top. Bootprints walk in and out of the pool. Even bare feet, every toe visible. Something small and red lies on one corner of the platform, prevented from rolling off the slanted surface by a knot of wood. As I sidle closer, breath held, in case someone is coming up behind me (or

around me, in the fog) or (God forbid) *underneath* the platform somehow, oh my God, my heart couldn't take it, I see
that it's just a finger. I thought it might be something worse.

A pinky, I think. He had very small hands, whoever he was.

It's over. I am glad I did not see or hear it. Obscurely, I am
also glad that Henryk didn't.

Not that we haven't seen things. Only that once, generally,
is plenty.

I wonder what they do in the domes if they catch someone
like this. Or do things like this simply not happen there? No,
they must have a system. People are people wherever you go;
and they aren't any better than us.

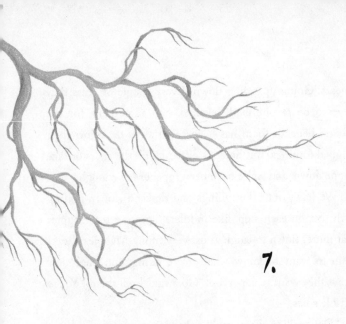

7.

By the time I meet Henryk over by the Drop, I am tired and cranky from the morning's work and skipping lunch. He doesn't look like he's faring much better. First things first we must get that out of the way.

"You look like shit," I tell him.

"You too. And you need a haircut. That rat's nest."

"What, so I can look like you?"

"You *wish*," he says loftily, because I have walked into it, "you could look like me."

"Up yours."

"Up what, I always wonder," he says. "I mean, *yours* could be anything."

"I don't know. It's just such a mom thing to say. So it must be something really terrible."

The stairs down to the valley gleam in the long afternoon light, soft-edged gold, two lanes marked in dark parallel smears. Going up, going down. Every couple of years they have to be re-plumbed, levelled, and shored up, for the ground beneath them has been eaten away far below their original footings. But here it's either climb the stairs or take a rope down, and we've both been ropeburned enough.

We hang onto the railings and descend slowly, putting both feet on each step, like toddlers, ignoring the magpies that flutter down to laugh at us. Very funny. Magpies always seem to want to know what you're doing; and once they know, they want to supervise. "Go away," I tell them. "You're terrible spies."

"Don't talk to them, you'll only encourage them."

"Where did you read that?"

"Some old lady told me. I don't *just* read, you know."

We wind between stumps and saplings, step through dogwood, rose, handsy willow, batting away the light branches, dried-out and stiff from the long winter. Sap has not risen yet, and the few inches of remaining soil are still frozen above the bedrock. Strong sweet musk of last fall's leaves, exposed by the melting snow and forming slick rugs under our careful feet. A smell of childhood. Running wild in the dust and the smoke, sliding on these leaves in the understorey. Patches of snow remain in the shade, dirty brown and grey, but the droplets that melt from the icy trees are impossibly clear, sparkling and catching the sun and flying into our upturned faces like rain.

"What did you bring?" I ask.

"Sling, spear. You?"

"I found a couple of arrows, but they're all shit. From two summers ago. Remember when McKinnon had that workshop thing and we all made like a hundred of them?"

I glance at the bow on his back, white PVC like mine, smudged with grimy fingerprints. The string doesn't look too good, but I guess if his arrows are shit too it won't matter. Mostly, I think, we came to get our legs back under us. Like going back to sea.

"It's funny," he begins, "because, like, back then . . ."

"They didn't even *eat* rabbit. You never see it in the cookbooks."

"Yeah. And if you wanted one you could just shoot it with a gun."

Back then, back then. Back then and their guns. We don't even know what we mean exactly when we say *back then*, or Back Then, capitalized, like Anno Domini; what time period, in years. Yash and Maliah's long-ago girlhood. Before Cad. Before the ultrastorms — the Big One and then the next Big One and then the next and the next and the next, often but not always roaring into the river valley like a giant stubbing his toe and collapsing into impotent rage and debris on our side. They didn't cause the end of everything, we figured; everything was ending anyway. But neither is it very clear what did cause the rift between Back Then and now. So much burned and blew away, leaving no trace, like a carcass that did not fossilize.

As we mine out the landfills (at least they left us a lot of plastic to reuse; that was thoughtful) and burrow into basements and archives seeking the books that our ancestors did not burn to survive the winters, you feel it sometimes, rage filling you like an updraft of hot air from a fire, lifting you from the shoulders or blowing through you like a tornado — rage that we missed it, missed it all, and rage at those who got to have it in the specific way that took it from us.

And we don't even know what *it* is. Only that we want to get back to it, and we never will, because they made that impossible. What has been broken has been broken in a way that can no longer be fixed.

Reading about it all in novels: smartphones, internet, satellites, the ISS, movies, cruises, road trips, texting, trains, flying in planes over countries with the cloud shadows moving dark and wet over the land like ink; but also all the things they wrote in there that they did not mean to write about because they were too normal, letting us look at them from the corner of their eyes. Restaurants. Rice. Dumpsters. Condoms. Bosons. Irrigation. Pensions. Bananas.

I think: My fucking Christ, imagine a world where you could fear *flying*.

Henryk feels it too, the rage I mean, the upward pull of it, when you know there's no starting over. When you know that everything we needed to start over was thrown away or burnt up decades before we were born. We can't have any of that.

Maliah told me: *They said to us, We'll keep the lights on as long as we can. And they did. You could flip a switch and at least there was light. We could not run our stoves or our fridges but light, always light. Then brownouts, then blackouts. The panels broke and no one could fix them. No more diesel for generators and no more coming. Click, click, click.* (Her long beautiful willow-gold hand gesturing at the dead switch on the wall.) *Till finally we all had to admit nothing was coming back on. It was dark always. Now, babies crawl around without fear and put their tongues into the sockets like there is milk inside.*

I hadn't understood every single word in that story (diesel, for instance: that was clothes, wasn't it?), but I had understood enough. Back Then, they had built things you couldn't fix when they broke. The time to be angry at them for doing so is long over. And the world burned anyway: and there was no water to put it out, nor will to carry a bucket. And those with the water hid themselves and it away and pretended the flames did not exist.

That's where I'm going, though, I think. To a place where they hoarded that water. I wonder if this is part of reparations, or just guilt. If they are doling it back out too late — spurred by pity or charity or morbid curiosity — to those who burned.

Henryk has not noticed my woolgathering, as I stare at his bow, joggling unevenly on his back as we pick our way down to the trails. "What about here?" He gestures at a low, dark clearing, cluttered with dogwood. A few thin shoots of grass have begun to sprout, startling green against the snow. The rabbits have had nothing good to eat in months; bark, maybe lichen. They'll want fresh grass. I decide to take its presence as a good omen.

We cast our eyes to the ground, looking for their neat round poops. The North Sask is as high as it'll ever be — with the glaciers gone, it's mostly snowmelt now, and the occasional rain. It will not approach the banks so closely for the rest of the year. The sound is soothing, like the wind through the bare branches, still dripping icemelt on us. I glance around for clear icicles and break off a couple to suck on, the water so pure it tastes sweet to the tongue.

"I don't really want a rabbit," I tell him, chewing on the ice. "I want a bucket of maple syrup."

"Me too," Henryk says around his. "I'm tired of vegetables. I want sweets."

"Oh, but we *need* vegetables to grow big and strong!" I chirp in my best Mrs. Cross voice.

"That was horrific," he whispers. "Uncanny. Please do not do that again."

"You think I'll scare the bunnies?"

"I'll let you know when my soul comes back to my body." He snaps off another icicle and gives it to me. "Here. Don't talk."

We circle the clearing, finding a couple different types of shit, all old, and no prints. Down the trails, then, closer to the water. Here you can smell the river's breath, fast and clean, drowning out the heavy scent of the rotting leaves. It doesn't smell like spring yet, but it does smell like thaw. See it through the trees: blackly glittering through two cliffs of stubborn ice. More green here, sprouting on the edges of the narrow foot trails, tiny wheatgrass and thick strappy crabgrass, some nibbled down. "There we go."

The air is still, the ground emanating cold. We squat in a tangle of willow, find canes to take our weight. Behind us rattles and clicks, like the beginning of a song. For all the stillness, clouds curdle and race across the sky. "Look how fast they're going."

"I hope it rains later." Henryk glances around for another icicle, and clucks in exasperation.

"Don't say that. It'll be harder to hunt."

He glances at me. "Is your mom really mad at you?"

"No."

"Oh. Because for a minute there I thought . . ."

I let him think it. We sit in the willow bush and listen to the breeze in the frozen forest. In the old days, we would have pointed upwards, made little wagers on which cloud would reach the top of the Stantec tower first, across the valley. Now of course we are too old for that. People our age are already getting married, finding new offices to live in, playing house.

He too could do whatever he wanted. No parents to tell him not to. No guilt, no shame. No mom to accuse him of laziness, disloyalty. Faithlessness. *Turning your back on your only family*: no one will say that of him. Hantavirus, a long terrible time of it, maybe a week, two weeks. Ripped through campus like a tornado, even though they said you couldn't pass it from person to person. Eighty dead at the end. Too many for our deadworkers, who collapsed, exhausted, napping upright against buildings and leaning on trees. And Henryk suddenly an orphan at fifteen. The great disaster, a child outliving his parents, both at once, no warning; he had gotten it too, but recovered. His hand on my sleeve at the memorial. We could not bring ourselves to embrace.

But you were done being parented at fifteen anyway, I had told myself, and meant it. Done with that complicated two-step of guilt, duty, love, obedience, and adulation; ready to join greater society as an adult, source of knowing instead of sink. And anyway we had all been raised just as much by each other, and our neighbours, our dozens of teachers, the caretakers in the big communal daycare, the river, the birds. The black and the green and the blue.

"I was up late reading." Henryk stifles a yawn in the crook of his elbow, and slowly unhooks his bow. "How come you didn't sleep?"

"I wasn't up late. I was up early. I wanted to go look at the platform in quad."

"Oh. When I went before work, it was down already. Did they hang the guy?"

"I don't think so. There was a lot of blood. Didn't the Flags give you anything to put up in the store?"

"No, nothing."

"Christ." Unbidden, my thoughts are again of my mother: all up in McKinnon's face, a foot and a half shorter than him, thrusting her finger at his beard. *Who took that confession? Who wrote it down?* She thought that mattered. The Flags, very clearly, did not. "What were you reading about?"

"Just Cad. The history and stuff. Did you know Mrs. Montpelier has a whole library about it? Nothing else."

"No, I didn't know that."

"In the Chem building. I had to pay for the lantern, but the books you can look at any time for free so long as you don't take them outside. There's some really interesting stuff in there."

"Mm." Does Mrs. Montpelier have Cad? I can't remember. There was a time when I kept a kind of running list in my head of people I knew to have it, updated as their diagnoses were confirmed (particularly during that hanta outbreak, when I had noticed that no Cad people had caught it) and again as people died of it. But now there are too many.

We are talking, I remind myself, not about some obscure medical curiosity but about me. *My* disease. What lives in *me*. Not an academic exercise, something we wrote papers on in school (though we did, in grade six and again in grade eight). But it still seems so distant. I look down at my thumbnails in the shade of the branches, as if in the last two minutes I have been suddenly cured. Nope. There they are: the tiny trees. One seems to shift subtly, like the kick of a fly's leg. I look away at once. Please don't remind me that you're in there. Let me pretend I'm alone.

Henryk says, "Remember, they said it started in Europe, and then vanished for a couple of years, and then popped up everywhere? Or it looked like everywhere? And everyone said it was being released from the melting permafrost —"

"Or bioweapons or whatever."

"Yeah. Or a lab accident. Or a government experiment. I mean people thought it was definitely bioengineered, and it was the Russians."

"Everybody thought everything was the Russians," I say. "That's literally the only thing I got from most of grade eight."

"Except the Russians, who thought everything was China."

"And the Chinese, who thought everything was the Americans."

"I wonder whatever happened to America," he says, then shakes his head, briskly, getting back to his secret library visit. "Anyway, I found out some people thought it was aliens. From a meteor that fell in Latvia. A really big one. The book had a picture, it was all burnt up from going through the atmosphere, but it was still as big as a car."

I think about Latvia, the modest blob of green on the globe, bounded by faded sepia lines. One in a million shot, with the gigantic pink swath of Russia just next door. "Some aim."

"Yeah. And then there was another theory that it was because the oceans were getting so hot, and some deep-sea fish with it came up to where they weren't supposed to and spread it into fish that people were eating."

"And heat doesn't kill the spores."

"Exactly. Exactly."

Nothing kills it. They taught us that, too. They tried chemotherapy, radiation, antibiotics, antivirals, predatory fungi, bacteria, phages. Dialysis: swapping old blood for new. Blood substitutes, even. People tried to burn it out, cut it out, starve it out. And died: either from bloodloss or shock, or the symbiont reacting somehow, thrusting itself into bones and nerves, closing around organs like a vise, when it had once wrapped them in the most delicate filigree. Once you have it, you have it. Forever.

"It doesn't matter where it came from," I say slowly.

"No, I mean of course it doesn't. I just keep thinking about it. I mean, this . . . thing. Alien thing. Deep-sea thing. On top of everything else."

"Yeah. Timing."

"Timing, exactly. The scientists thought it was adaptive at first," he says, making a conscious effort not to look at me. "A vestige from its original host. But it became maladaptive when it spread into people."

"Understatement of the century."

"The last of it, the last of the research, was about the hyphae," he says quietly. "They were trying to characterize what it makes. What it put into the bloodstream."

Hen, I want to say, even before he's finished, don't. Don't. Instead I stare wide-eyed at the ground, trying to find patterns in the leaves like you'd find in the clouds.

"Toxins, a ton of toxins, stuff that looked like snake venom, spider venom, fish endotoxins. A lot of small molecules and proteins that resemble neurotransmitters. They figured that's how it controls people's muscles once the infection gets past a certain point. Preferential, uh, what do you call it. Receptor/substrate pathways. They shout louder than your own chemicals. Cool, huh?"

"Mmph."

"It just means nerve," he says hastily, glancing at me. "Neuro. It doesn't mean brain. It doesn't mean —"

"But they didn't look at that. Did they."

"I . . . I don't know. The book didn't say."

My knee begins to jiggle nervously on its own, as if I were sitting in class; I quell it with an effort. "Howse must have figured out a better test. More accurate."

"Yeah."

"I thought maybe they cured it, I thought . . . maybe people don't die of it there. I . . ."

He nods, reaches over, puts the back of his wrist on mine for a second. "I keep thinking about Nads. How proud she'd be of you for getting in. How she would have loved your essay."

Oh God. The name unspoken for years. Sweeter to the tongue than ice. A wrench to the heart: gentle, lovely Nadiya, who had always been with us, the third side of our triangle, who at thirteen was diagnosed with Cad and had it go off within three months of those first faint green markings. Fucking hell, and it had seemed so hugely terrifying back then, and unfair, unjust, that you should be beautiful and good and die screaming, distorted beyond recognition, even the face all wrong, the skull all wrong. When the clumsily refined products of our minimal, hardy-zone poppy harvest could no longer quell the pain, her family took her to Calgary to die. Gone in the middle of the night. No goodbyes.

All the shit we had managed to get up to. The kitten ranch. The arrow business. Our air band, complete with hand-cranked record player. That time we climbed the High Level Bridge across to the Legislature and picked excitedly amongst the crumbling ruins, dodging a sudden stonefall by mere seconds. That should have been years, decades, a lifetime together. Nads and her big deer eyes with their impossibly long, silky lashes, like feathers.

It occurs to me that if she had not gotten sick, she probably would have been the one to get into the university. They would have wanted her so badly. If anyone. Not me. Her.

"I miss her. It's bullshit that she isn't here for this," I say.

"It is. I know." The wind picks up; he buttons his jacket to the top, cringing further into the willow for the little shelter it gives. "I think I was in love with her."

"I don't blame you," I say, casually, though the shock of it rocks me back on my feet for a second, ending, like the aftermath of a tornado, in a sick, dark little twirl in my stomach, a small storm destroying a few last buildings; I feel lightheaded. Don't be an asshole. For fuck *sake*. We were all kids together, kids get crushes, and she was beautiful, remember that? And what is beautiful these days but each other? So graceful. Her laughter, that held nothing back. Henryk in love with her: come on. Like you know what the word means at that age. It doesn't mean anything. And so what, anyway? It's just Henny. It's not like . . . Stay casual. Don't pause too long. "You never told her?"

"I was going to. Then I couldn't. I thought maybe . . . I don't know." He waves a hand listlessly, staring down at the river. "Girls, right? Thought maybe I'd get you to tell her. Then I thought that was a stupid idea. I mean. What, I couldn't talk to her myself? The three of us talked to each other like twenty hours a day."

"Yeah. Stupid idea. Glad you didn't do it." Still, my stomach spins; I feel gross, even a little nauseated. I wish I had more ice to chew. I pick off a willow twig and stick it between my back teeth: acrid taste of chemical sap. You'd have to chew a bushel of it to relieve this level of pain, but my tongue is momentarily distracted.

"Mom would have been so happy. I kept thinking that. She loved Nads. She would have loved for her to be, like, part of our family or whatever. When we were older."

"Everybody loved her. It's not fair, that . . . " I give up, shrug. We've said it all before. Everyone did. Nothing's fair. Nothing's ever been fair. And nothing (this is the really important part) ever will be.

Long minutes pass in silence. There: something rangy hopping downslope into view. For a second it is as if the undergrowth has come alive, the grey of dead leaves and grass, but no, it's a rabbit all right. Uncaring of us, maybe because it cannot smell us yet. Human voices are a distant thing to it, probably. Not a threat. Or maybe because we are down here so infrequently that generations and generations have told themselves that we aren't a threat. Not really.

It's about thirty paces away. Stealthily, Henryk raises his bow, then grimaces in dismay. Knew it from looking at it: needs restringing. He won't get enough draw to skewer a boiled potato.

I heft my spear instead. I'm no good with it, but at this distance it should barely matter, and I slot it delicately into its holder and rise to a crouch so my arms don't get tangled in the willows. Inhale. Sight. You don't want to tag it in the ass, because it'll just take the hit in muscle and bolt to escape the pain. The head, or the back of the neck, that's what you want. No pain to run from. Just darkness.

Something flickers in the corners of my vision. Branches? Bugs? Like eyelashes, but weightless, without colour. Have to ignore it to aim, everything crisp for a moment, bright and sharp, even the sun moving obligingly from behind a galloping cloud, the rabbit oblivious, munching, hunched, and everything as still as a drawing.

Draw back. Line up shoulder and hip. Release.

The rabbit flattens with hardly a sound, only the solid *chunk* of the thick glass point crashing into the bones of the spine. For a second I cannot even believe it worked — surely I fucked up, and it will rise, and scream, and stagger around in the half-eaten grass, spurting blood. But no, it's well and truly down, and Henryk whoops.

"Shit yeah! Hail Nimrod, mighty hunter!"

"Whaaat the shit! First shot!"

"I'll go grab it," he says, and hands me his bow, and slides down the slope. And then several things happen at once.

Even before the shapes flow out of the trees, there is something spilling into my eyes, dark first then bright, so that it seems the sun has focused all its rays on the gilded painting that is now being composed by the sure hand of a master: *Boy, Rabbit, Dogs*.

"Hen! Hey!"

He is watching his footing on the slick grass, only looks up at my shout. Everything seems to be stuck, jittering. Too slow. Realization dawns on his face at the speed of a real dawn, light cresting the horizon for hours; the sprinting ferals seem to run through cobwebs. Teeth bared. Ribs bared too, like a second set of jaws embedded in their mangy skin.

They lunge for the rabbit at first, and then — visibly, with the full thrill of anticipation and delight expressed in dog body language — realize that bigger prey is steps away.

I drop the bow, begin to run for him. I make it one step before something inside me locks — slams shut like a door, freezing me in place. For breath after breath I can only watch, terrified, paralyzed, as one dog, black with yellow spots, seizes the rabbit and worries it in its jaws, and another, coyote-gold, leaps for Henryk, knocking him onto his back so they disappear into the bush. A despairing yell, the crunch and clatter of breaking branches. And I can't move and he's alone and this has never happened before and —

No. Fuck you and the fucking hyphae you rode in on. Fuck you, *fuck you*, and through first immobility and then agony, like running with a charley horse in every limb, I force one foot to move, the other, nerves on fire. I shove myself down the slope, wade into the dogs, keeping my hands far from their snapping jaws. Screaming mostly in pain, but hoping to scare them too, arms waving, grabbing the dropped spear, jamming it into faces and open jaws, running-sliding for Henryk, who is shrieking under a mass of fur and mange and about two steps from tumbling onto the rotten ice of the river.

Groaning with effort, it is like something inside me burning away, a little puff of kindling disappearing in the fire, fighting against the darkness that I have only tempo-rarily driven back from its rightful claim. The spear tip breaks with a high, sharp note that sends a couple dogs yelping away, but I wade in anyway, slapping and stabbing, till Henryk can struggle to his feet.

The pack disperses at last, seeing us upright as a united threat. By the time we claw our way back up the slope, I expect the rabbit to be gone, but it remains, harried a little, next to the green ice glint of the broken spearpoint. One dog lies nearby, still weakly thrashing. We give it a wide berth.

We are soaked in thin mud, Henryk is shivering, his jacket hood filled with snow. All my muscles hurt as if I've been hauling bricks. Back, neck, legs, where I forced them to move against the will of the nameless invader. They've never had to work that way. Walking is a struggle, but we have to get out of here.

"W-wuh-we should put it out of its, uh, its muh-misery," Henryk manages, looking at the dog. It's a particularly nasty specimen, black and pink and half-skinless, nearly lipless, the teeth exposed and shining, so sharp they too look like the broken edge of my spear. It must have been very hungry to come at us like that. Or maybe not. We're not so big. And there were ten or twelve of them. We need to start moving in a pack, I almost say.

I don't know if I can kill it, with my spear tip broken. The sling won't do any good at such close range. An arrow, maybe, into one of the big veins of the neck? But I don't want to get close enough for it to snap at me. I'm shuddering, my teeth chattering. "Where did that phrase come from, anyway. Misery. Why not something else."

"Ennui."

"Weltschmerz."

"What does that mean?"

"I don't know. I read it in a novel."

I suppose it'll have to be an arrow. I take one from Henryk's quiver then stop dead: the dog's body ceases trembling as we watch, the bony back legs kick out — once, twice — and it falls still. But there is still movement within it: deep, deep within, where

(where the being lives, the manythreaded monster, where it lives dark and green and held you back, where it said don't go, it's not safe, let him die, deep in that place, that same place)

the guts might be trying to expel a tapeworm, something, a

(parasite say it)

denizen shocked by the sudden ruination of its home, all the lights going out. The side heaves, the dry gritty hairs standing up on end like dead trees, and then something small bursts between two ribs, half an inch, an inch, a blink and it is as long as my hand, a tiny bluish fern, swelling at the top. Not blooming. Not exactly. A fat swelling, fleshy, foreign flesh, chitin-looking, iridescent green and black. Mushrooming. Oh my fucking God.

I grab Henryk's arm. "Run. Go!"

"But —"

My shove catches him in the small of the back so that he falls, swearing, but then he's up and dashing back towards the stairs. I snatch the rabbit, getting closer than I want to the sprouting monstrosity, which waves in the still air as if sniffing, scenting, pausing to face me — the swelling as big as my fist now, emitting a slow stream of smoky spores but giving every impression that it's about to burst.

And then I'm gone too, arms pumping, a straight shot up the stairs where Henryk's muddy white jacket is a beacon guiding me home.

We stagger back in silence. My thighs burn from the stairs and from the work of fighting my temporary paralysis; Henryk is wheezing. The stupid, skinny, ragged rabbit hangs from my fist. In the shadow of our home we stop and collapse against the wall. I want to scream.

It's never done that before. I had read about it, even half-believed it, but I had never truly experienced what Cad could do — that sickening grip inside, the instant fear, as if someone had thrust a bag over my head. Nothing I've felt in my life could have compared to it. No secret internal movements with their own agendas — cramps, hunger pangs, the clutch and release of my monthly blood. There are so many muscles in the body we cannot control. I know that. It should have been familiar. A little.

But to have it confirmed: that yes, there are things the disease does not want you to do, and no, you will not be able to do them. And that it might do this again. That it *will* do it again. That it is getting worse: that this is a slide towards whatever it wants to do next. And not what I want to do. Stay safe, it says. I will make you safe. No matter what.

And the dead dog —

Henryk is staring at me, fearful. "Are you okay?"

"Fine. Ran too fast. Stairs."

"Thanks for coming to get me."

"Yeah. No prob. Like I wouldn't."

"Reid, listen though . . ." He casts around for a moment, trying to say something difficult. His gaze shoots down to the rabbit, to the ground, to my left shoulder, at last up to my eyes. "Your face . . ."

"What?"

"Go home," he says. "Go home and look."

"I . . . okay. I'll come bring you your share after I —"

"It's fine. Keep the whole thing. It's for you and your mom."

"Henryk."

"I'll talk to you later," he blurts, and takes off, half running.

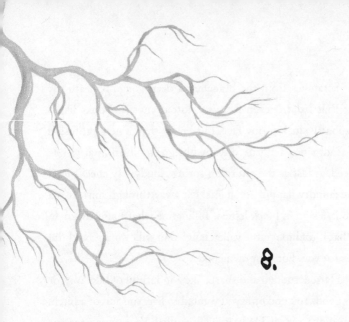

8.

Home is silent, half filled with sunset like weak tea. I trudge through the door, eel past the dividers without looking at them, begin to push open the door to my office. It moves in silence a few inches: just enough to see Mom, furtive, quick-moving, her hands busy in my small filing cabinet, opening the top drawer, shutting it, opening the second drawer, digging her hands into rags and underwear, shutting it.

I clear my throat.

Mom spins, too fast. "Hi, baby. What w— oh my God!"

"Um. I went to the valley? We got a rabbit, but uh . . . Kind of slipped in the mud."

She's not staring at my clothes, though. She's staring at my face. Still holding the rabbit, the battered claws of its hind legs digging into my palm, I push past her, gently, and take the tiny hand mirror from the top drawer of my filing cabinet.

Scratches from the branches, a deep gouge beneath my eye that I didn't even feel. It's clotted, mostly. Looks like a raspberry stuck to my face. But below that, a new profusion of Cad: vines, tendrils, dreamy bluegreens shifting at visible speed, as fast as the returning spring clouds. My cheeks look like laundry flapping on a line. Far away, through mist. It is a shout, a sign in block letters. Telling me what I already knew. What it told me in the valley, tangled in willows. It says, I did this for you. For your own good.

Hatred, sudden and sharp, like a mouthful of bile. *Not* for my good. You and only you wanted to live, you son of a bitch. You didn't care if Henryk lived or died. Worse: you *wanted* him to die if it meant you would survive.

I want to ask Mom about it over a mug of tea. Sit on the lab bench like we always do, forearms on the black plastic. Has it happened to you? Did you feel something move inside you? Were you afraid? Resigned? Did it feel like the kick of a baby: the motion of a foreign thing inside your body reminding you that a thing without a name lives inside you? Reminding you that you aren't alone?

She's shocked, worried. I wonder what it would be like to let her comfort me again. To try to be comforted. For a second I ache for it, like real hunger. How can I leave her? Who will comfort me when I am surrounded by strangers?

"I'll go take this apart." In response she comes forward and palpates the carcass briskly, without distaste for the dusty pelt, the obvious bite-marks from the dogs.

"Pretty scraggy."

"Yeah."

"If you get the hide off in one piece, though, they might be able to get *one* pair of mittens out of them for you. It's lucky you've got such small hands, for all your height."

"I could've been a surgeon, back then."

"Baby, you would have been a wonderful surgeon. Even now . . ." She trails off. The university seems to loom between us, shouldering us aside. But no: I will not stay here and train under our doctors on the fastest ways to hurt people. Even if it was her dream. She could have told me.

The main thing, I want to tell her, is that you wake up from dreams.

I head back to the main lab and arrange a spot on the counter to skin and butcher the rabbit. A fiddly process, and I haven't done it for a while. Green lines are marching up my wrists like caterpillars, and at almost the same speed. I ignore them as I sharpen my knife, wash my hands.

Trying to concentrate, but my mind is running on a parallel track, harried and fluffed like a nesting bird: Did she check under my covers? Did she find my secret hiding spot? The cabinet was where I put all my childhood treasures — bits of petrified wood, a desiccated marten skull, a couple of magpie feathers — but the accepted agreement, never spoken, is that even though we have no secrets between us, and indeed she watched me bring in every item that was stored within it over the years, she would never open it to look, just as I never open her secret tins or boxes, stored on the lab shelves.

If she thought the whole thing was a hoax, why would she go for the letter and the tracker?

The knife slips; my hands jerk away from each other so sharply that the knife almost flies into the far wall. I steady my grip, heart pounding, and grimly continue. The blood helps after a few moments: slick at first, then sticky. Mom's eyes on me, as palpable as a touch.

"You should change your clothes. Have a bath."

"I cleaned my hands."

"The mud is flaking off."

"I'll be careful."

Without its pelt, the rabbit, a buck, is pathetically skinny. A hard winter, not very cold but seemingly neverending. I feel more sorry for it than other things I've hunted. It survived and survived and survived as its friends and family perished, and finally, when the worst was clearly and provably over, when a mouthful of grass could be felt between the teeth at last, no spring came.

Sorry, sorry, sorry. I hope you lived well. Sired kits. A little of you hops around still, I hope. The part of you that is unaware that it is from you.

Its flesh is clean though, no worms or pockets of infection. Not like us. A rabbit, killing and butchering me, would toss me away in disgust and scrub its paws with bleach. Imagine that, one day: generation after generation of Cad infected people having kids, living safely, leaving the risks to the others, till down the line everyone had it and we would finally be docile and wise as the fungus wished us to be. Everyone else dead. *Natural selection, bitches*, as Larsen would say. Cut us open: tree after tree, marked in black and green.

"You didn't go alone, did you?"

"No! No. God. Of course not. I went with Henryk. He didn't want his half. Good thing too, I mean look at this guy." I begin to part it out, making sure I keep everything away from the bowl of guts. Cut here, then here, then here, then here. Funny how it comes right back to you. Muscle memory.

"You know," she says, moving to the far end of the bench, "I hadn't even met your father when I was your age. People were getting married later then too. In their twenties. When they had gotten to know each other a little better."

"Mm." Hindquarters set aside, take off the loins: gently, pushing it up with the thumbs. Favourite part. Poach those in oil tonight and spoil ourselves away from the Dining Hall. Tired of eating lentils and beans and field peas all the time; sometimes you just want meat.

"My mother still thought that was too young, in fact. She married at thirty-three. She wanted me to be more independent first, find an office somewhere, live on my own for a while. *I don't want you to think your whole life relies on someone*, she used to say. *You need to learn how to be your own support*."

"Yeah."

"And I wasn't thinking about that while your father and I were going out. Of course. But I remembered it after he left and it was just you and me. Not that you weren't doing your best, baby, but you know. You were only six. I kept worrying: What would happen to us? Would we be okay? What will she think of marriage, when she gets older? What will she think about men? Because, you know, we only know what we've been taught. And we can only be taught what we see."

Another proverb she thinks she came up with, but I've heard the oldsters say it before her. I guess it fits, anyway. She thinks life is endless repetition, and that there's nothing wrong with it, and that's accurate. The same patterns writ small and large, always recognizable, even at a glance. You copy what you see in your family, which copies what it sees in its neighbourhood, which copies what it sees in its city.

"You know, Henny's a . . . he's a good boy. He's always been a good friend. I'm not saying he's a bad person . . ."

At last I stop and look up, bloodied to the wrists, stuck in place lest I drip on the floor. We stare at each other. Her gaze is righteous, defiant. Rimmed darkly with blue, her eyes seem larger and younger than I've seen them for years. Oh boy, here it comes.

". . . But you know, baby, people grow apart. Sometimes the people you like when you're young aren't . . . aren't the kind of people you'd necessarily be friends with when you're older. Because they have different values. Different priorities."

"I guess so."

"So I just want you to be sure, really sure, that if you think this . . . this university place . . . is real, and it's somewhere you want to go, that that's not something that people are . . . influencing you to think. Because sometimes a tempting idea gets more tempting with peer pressure. Especially if you're too . . . if you let yourself get too involved with someone. They can have a lot of influence on what you think. If you just stepped back and . . ."

"Mom, can you . . . *involved*? Involved *how*? What do you mean 'too involved'? I mean, can you just . . . help me out here, please, just say it if you think . . . Henryk and I are sleeping together or whatever. Because first of all we're not, and secondly, I can think for myself."

"I'm not saying you're not thinking for yourself! I'm just saying, sometimes people don't realize why they're thinking something, till they look at it by themselves and —"

"And even if I was banging someone —"

"Reid, I'd prefer if you used a less vulgar expression."

"What? All right, I don't know. If I was in love with someone, if I was — is that still too vulgar? If I was *involved* with someone, why would you think I wouldn't know my own mind? That's not how it works, that's not remotely what it means."

"You've never been in love, baby, it can be very intense, especially at your age — when you're older, you'll see what I mean —"

"Just because you lost your mind with a man doesn't mean it happens to everybody!"

We both stop midway through whatever we were going to say next, as if I had slapped her. The tears are close to the surface again. Even an apology will not take that back. I look down at the lab bench: bloodied lumps on the black. Like the platform, in the cold fog of the morning. And in fact, do the marks on her face look darker now? Even now, while we've been talking? As if I did slap her and left these instead of reddened skin.

Who's talking to me? Her, or her sickness?

Do you understand, I want to tell her, do you understand that I did not consent to this: to having Cad, to being born with it. That you forced that upon me. As your mother and father forced it upon you. Do you understand that I am angry? That my anger is the same as yours should have been? That I fear darkly that you want me to stay and it wants me to stay and I can't tell the difference between

(neurotransmitters. it doesn't)

(don't)

(it just means nerve it doesn't mean brain it doesn't mean)

(*stop it*)

(mind, it doesn't mean you, what you are, where you live)

I realize I'm panting, as if I've just run up the stairs. Flight after flight after flight after flight, no breaks. Not even sure what I'm mad about. Being accused of an untruth is one thing, but this is very mild. It is far worse that she thinks I don't *know* myself. Or that she is trying to talk me into not knowing myself. That she thinks Henryk has his thumb on some invisible scale in my heart, and that she too thinks she has a thumb on the scale.

But as soon as I think it, I feel sick, monstrous. Of course she does. And of course she should. She's my mother, my only family. Brought me into the world. Raised me alone. With love that has never wavered. Now I throw it back into her face. What we owe each other may not be precisely equal or even equitable, but it is not this.

With an effort, I slow my breath, and finish the rabbit, and wash my hands again, and pour the bloody water into our plants. "I'll take the bones down to the kitchen, unless you want them."

"No, go ahead. I'll deal with the meat."

"Thanks."

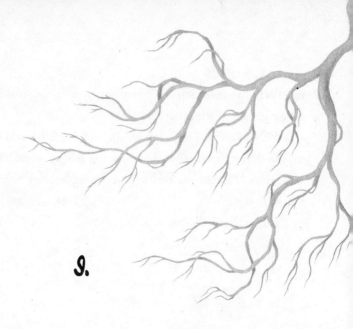

9

Two days remain till the pig hunt, forty-eight hours to build up a real good supply of adrenaline and have it gnaw away at my nerves; on the Wednesday morning I am temporarily recruited to help turn compost, which needs a lot of pitch-forks and a lot of backs. Warm work, hard to fuck up. For a few hours I manage to bed down my screeching brain and I listen eagerly to the gossip and flirting. But the minute I stop moving, my brain gets back to work on the only thing it seems to want to do right now: thinking of things that will go wrong during the hunt, and gruesomely playing them inside my head on a loop.

After lunch, I spin with Mom for a few hours, then wander back outside to look at our allotment. But this leaves me queasy and strangely disoriented, as if the ground is slowly revolving, and I cannot bear it for long. Maybe I am getting sick, I think as I walk. Maybe that rabbit was infected with something after all. Can't always tell can you. Not everything signs its name on your face like Cad does. I do feel feverish, I feel not just heated from exertion but simmering from within, a heat generated from what feels like my marrow.

From talking to people, it seems this is the time of year you might get a pig and not die. Now, when they've been hungry all winter, and might finally be getting weak. Watchful, yes, but slow and languid from the long starving. Better eats in the fall, absolutely, and Back Then I think people only did hunt in the fall, because they wanted to play fair, but we will not play fair, we cannot.

But Hen and I were worse than a joke during our rabbit hunt. We were a danger to each other and anybody around us, we were lucky to get out of there in one piece. And that was just the valley dogs!

I don't know what I can bring to the pig hunt. It's clear I can't *learn* anything to help myself before then, but good equipment might give me enough of an edge. Maybe the new makers will have something.

It is sunny, cold, a stiff breeze carrying a smell of snow rather than rain. I imagine the heat of my fever blowing off me like dust. Reaching Whyte, I take off my jacket and carry it flapping in one hand. Sometimes you can find things here that you can't find in the campus stores. Maybe I will know it when I see it.

Fat white clouds over the valley, blustering and important, on their way to some committee or other. Places to be. Not like me, wandering; my life (not that you say it out loud), what is required of me, is not so dangerous, not so hard. Not like those early days of starting over, when a living had to be scratched out of the dying earth. Something a teacher once said, about how as society progresses you can tell it is doing so by the amount of leisure time people have — the amount of time you are not literally trying not to starve.

With a little start I think of the story we were studying when that came up. What had it been called? Something very simple. The sweet and brainless Eloi, who did nothing but eat and dance and sing, and then the horrible Morlocks, who lived underground and ate flesh (could you call them cannibals if the species had diverged so much? I had written an essay about it, and failed, and to add insult to injury earned a *See me after class* for apparent pro-cannibal tendencies). What if it was like that in the domes? Had it been long enough? Probably not, three or four generations, and yet — Eloi alone had gone into them, sort of. Would they look at me and see a Morlock?

I stop at some random storefront, not really hearing the patient ringing hammerblows from within. Was that what the universities were doing? Taking in a feral pet, taming it, hoping for . . . what? Civilization? A terrible idea, a terrible word. Civilization is a word from Back Then — a noun meaning something that had destroyed itself because that is what civilizations were meant to do, and a verb meaning "to ruin by extraction." Rich places sending our trash to poor ones so they could pick through it for recyclables, like we do now. Always people have simply lived the way they thought they should based on what was around. They threw away plastic, understanding that it would never be needed again. And now we cannot make it, so we use what they left us. The Indigenous people here under centuries of colonizers, till we broke the world and they quietly, nearly overnight, packed up and left the cities together, to live better on the land that their invaders were too busy dying and fighting to lay claim to any longer.

A few had stayed, and rarely spoke about those who had left, always with a kind of dreamy dismissiveness — assurances that it was better out there. We told ourselves: That cannot be. You can't live except in a city. They can't start over out there. Later, I thought: But you don't need a clean slate, do you? That's not why they left. They already knew that. Just a slate is enough. Remembering that for Europeans it was not enough that we barged in to infect, to occupy, but that we invaded with violence, the intent to *possess* the "new" continent in a way that the people already living there did not. Destroy, steal, poison, rename, kill, barricade, and deny. In every way like Cad, the colonizer that should not have lived in us, should never have left whatever creature foul or fair it belonged in, but came anyway to possess, not to cohabit. Well then, maybe this is our punishment for that. But how does a fungus know who to punish?

I pass the places that pass on treasures: a glass smelter, plastic warehouse, places offering compressed waste pellets to burn in stoves and boilers, a charcoal burner with beautifully labelled tins of tooth powder. Here I hesitate: The letter didn't say what to bring to Howse. Would I need to provide my own toiletries? Sheets? Towels? My God. I don't even know what classes I'll be taking. I was accepted into Environmental Science. What will that mean?

If it was a real university, wouldn't they tell me those things?

I've hesitated too long, frozen in doubt; the lady inside lures me in, and insists I get an Original Mint tooth powder even though I don't have any store tokens or barter on me. I put my name in her book and put the tin in my breast pocket. "I'll send a runner to collect later in the week," she says. "Look after your teeth! You only get one set."

"Yes'm."

Dazed, anxious, I wander back out. Workshops now more than storefronts, people repairing wheelchairs and crutches, building steamcarts, scooters, gliders (oh no: I've always wanted a glider, and it is too late to save up for one now), water filters. A heavy, savoury smell draws me to an open doorway, a blast of strangely organic heat. Not like the heat from a fire, but almost animal — like the breath of good compost. It smells like a bakery, overlaid with a piercingly sour scent. I pause on the threshold. Vampires, wasn't it? You had to invite them in.

"Hello?" someone calls, a high clear voice. A young woman comes out, wiping her hands on a rag; she is semi-familiar to me for some reason. Maybe a couple of years ahead of me in school. I don't remember her name, but she cries, "Reid, isn't it? How are you? Are you hungry?"

"No! I just, um. The scent carries all the way down the block."

She beams. Her cheeks are gold-brown and flawless, but I see the marks of the nameless marching up her neck, green and blue. Hello, sister.

She says, "New batch. Want to come try?"

"New batch of what?"

I follow her into the back of the workshop, the smell growing heavier and damper by the minute, and we emerge at last into a plastic-sheeted courtyard full of the spring's thin sun. A couple of teenagers diligently decant something from large, dented tanks, while an older woman and a big man in a leather apron play chess on a chalked-up tabletop. It takes me a minute to realize it's a still of some kind — or no, bigger than that. What's the word?

"A brewery," the woman says helpfully. I wish I could remember her name, but the older man solves that for me by springing to his feet when we come in.

"Jamie!"

"Just giving a sample to Brains here," she says, and I flush automatically: I don't know how the news got off campus, but here we are.

"It's *bad* for brains," he says severely, and looks down at the board. "See?"

"It's not because you drink," his opponent says. "It's because you're terrible at chess."

We leave them bickering, and Jamie gets me a tumbler from one of the teenagers. *Distillery*, that's the word I'm looking for. The drink in the cup is bright, bready, bubbly. I sip it cautiously.

"That's our best so far. We've been experimenting with beer for a couple of years and haven't even got it to the same level as the ancient Egyptians. It's the water, you know? We have to be so careful with it, it kind of . . . knocks the life out of things."

"It's awesome."

"Thanks for saying so, but we can do better. Here, finish that." She refills my empty cup from a smaller tank, nudging away a white-and-brown dog lapping from the puddle below it. "Hops! For God's sake, don't drink that. Anyway, this is our cider. My personal favourite."

The cider is not better, but different; sweeter, sharper. I sip and look around at the complicated plastic tubing, the salvaged tanks scoured and polished, dozens of neat ceramic and glass bottles, bags of what I assume are raw materials. I'm sweating from the heat of fermentation. There's moonshine on campus, of course; you couldn't stop people from brewing booze if you tried. If the world had ended in atomic war instead of weather, there would still be someone crawling out of the irradiated slag to start a still. But half the time the campus stuff blinds you or makes you puke your guts out, so they use it at the hospital to disinfect tools and the rest of us steer clear. This is probably much safer, and clearly less explosive.

"You must be so excited," she says, peering at me over her own cup. "I mean, the university. That's so amazing. I sent in my application with Mrs. Cross too, but, well . . ."

"Yeah. It's all just . . . still so new, you know?"

The old man gets up, cursing quietly at the chessboard, and comes over with a white ceramic jug prominently labelled *SMITH*. I have figured out the pattern by now though, the smaller the bottle the higher the octane, and he proposes an academic toast with the contents — some kind of ultra-distilled cider that goes down like fire — and by the time I extricate myself, I am, I dimly realize, a little bit drunk for the first time in my life.

Delight. You read about it, but you don't know what it's like until you do it. Like other things. You can try to tell people what having Cad is like but they will never feel anything inside them like we feel. They will feel alone, like you're supposed to. Not occupied. Now, I feel doubly, triply occupied: hot, light-footed, everything with a pleasant aura around it in rainbowy spikes. If you drink beer and cider and (for lack of a better word) schnapps, what does the fungus drink? Funny to think it's off the clock now.

Well, this won't help with the hunt, though it's helping with my nerves, but that's not going to last. Anxiety still hums under the heavy blanket of booze: Will Koda tell me what to do? What if I die before I ever get to Howse?

And just as I think this I see something I have not seen before: a steeple, rising impossibly behind a derelict apartment building, just the tip of it peeking out, the cross scratched black against the sky. This must be investigated, of course, in case a god, the one whose name I regularly take in vain perhaps, remains there waiting for a single worshipper.

The building itself is low, grungy cream-coloured brick scribbled over with graffiti; the entire back wall is missing, so that the overall structure is only three sides and a roof. I enter through the front door anyway, because it seems like something they would have wanted me to do. As I pull the door open a snipped chain slithers from the handles, disintegrates at my feet in a puff of rust. I walk through the small heap of dead iron and into the shell of the church, gracefully arched where the outside is sharply angled. These were the timbers that could not be destroyed by storms or fires and were too big to loot. If a god is in here, I cannot yet hear it; I stop, and theatrically cock a hand to my ear, and laugh. It would echo, probably, if that back wall was there. Now, it just flies outside like a sparrow.

I pick a little unsteadily (whoops: those last two shots of concentrated apple) through the broken bricks and cement, the pews bolted to the floor. It's a small church, not like the big one downtown. New, maybe, built to fill a gap near the end when materials could still be had from overseas and people wanted a place to beg for salvation. Like you couldn't do it in your house. Maybe you couldn't.

I don't know anyone who prays now. No atheists in foxholes, they say, but maybe we are. Nadiya's parents, I remember, had prayed. Five times a day, pointed to . . . where? I couldn't remember the name of the city. But Nads herself had not, or she said she didn't. Her parents were quiet about it. Didn't push her. *You have to believe*, they said, *not just go through the motions; so if you don't believe, you should not, and we will not make you.* But she must have prayed at the end. How could you feel such pain and not cry out for the god of your ancestors?

My stomach gurgles warningly. Don't think about that. I trip over a pew, catch myself in a graceless half-twist. Everything feels easy, as if weights had been attached to my limbs and now they are gone. And from my new position I see an impossible — literally, I think — gleam of light and colour above me. A stained glass window. How? I have never seen one up close. Never looked through one. Immediately I am consumed not by a desire but a *need* to do so, and there remains a wooden staircase with a strip of dark green carpet running up the centre, and anyway the booze is probably wearing off, and I untangle myself from the pew and set off at half a run.

God wants me to look at this. God wants me to see those colours, weakly shining onto the opposite wall's crumbling white stucco. Royal blue and dark roses and greens, a gold like sunset. We use the word gold to mean a certain colour even if we have never seen the actual metal in our entire lives. I want to see it.

And just as I put a foot on the first step, I don't want to anymore.

Slowly, I back away: two paces, three, five. And the desire re-emerges with all the fire of those first moments. Something cold and sick snakes its way up from my gut. You, it's you, isn't it?

I try again and again: eyes open, eyes closed. On all fours, making my way up the ancient carpet nearly halfway before my body simply marches me back down. The fear surprises me; I can tell myself a hundred times that it is not real, but my internal shouting is the lone voice of dissent when my glands, my muscles, my gut, my disease, tells me it is.

So. That's how it is, is it. The thing in me feels the fear, and it says: *No, you cannot do that.*

Not, Don't do that. Not, I'd prefer if you didn't. But, *No.*

At last, exhausted, I sit on the floor and stare up at the small slice of window I can see from this level. The staircase sways in the wind. But I know I could have made it up there. Anger: the infection still lets me feel that. If I had doubted that the Cad was worsening, that doubt is gone. Nothing changes. Nothing changes except for the worse.

A god does not live here, or if there is one, it mocks me in silence; because it will not help me, and it will not end my pain and my fury. If you see something like this and you do nothing, then all you are doing is laughing, and with evil. The world isn't fair, the world isn't fair, they tell us that all the time. All the time. I think it was the first thing I learned to write.

I am not angry at god. But people must have been, back then. Mustn't they? To watch everything they loved and treasured and deemed beautiful and good fall apart around them; even if half or more of those things were caused directly by what they were doing, they must have wondered why a god had caused the others, and had not intervened, and had watched in silence. Here, a city of over a million where barely one in a hundred had survived the days of darkness. Cold, silent, dry. Dusty hands clasping over elephant bones in the zoo. And the first lesson they passed to their children: It isn't fair.

I wonder if it is fair under a dome. If they pray there.

A god does not live here, I tell myself again and again. A god does not live here. It is not a god I am leaving behind. Looking down at my nails: You are not a god. You are the only thing I hate.

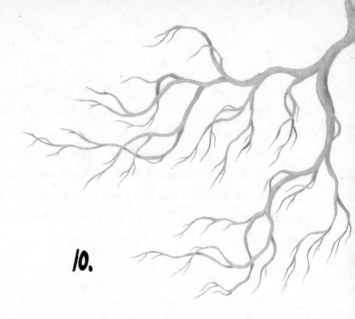

10.

I finish my Friday chores on Thursday, and before hauling myself to bed leave an enormous pile of finished yarn under a sheet. I suppose this is by way of a will — not that I have anything to leave, but we studied wills in school, one teacher even made us analyze a transcript of Shakespeare's will, and it is something that you are supposed to have if you are a grownup. Even if all it says is "I have nothing."

I tried to get you a little ahead of the curve, is what the pile says. It is also, I suppose, a farewell note: as opposed to the real note I left, which says that I am headed to help Koda at the soapworks. I glance at the heap only once on Friday morning as I leave the house, silently, in my good boots.

We didn't have much weaponry in the house. Unable to ask around about weaponry, not wanting to reveal the time or day of the hunt, I'd had to scrounge from people under other pretexts: spears I'd had to make in the middle of the night from knives borrowed from the kitchen, the rabbit farmers. "I'll bring it right back," I said, once, twice, three times. I hoped it was true.

Now, as I leave, I pause and listen. I have carefully strapped everything against myself so I can grab it easily, and so it does not jingle as I walk. All sharpened for hours, unblooded. I don't want to spook our pig.

They say a pig can smell like you wouldn't believe. Better than a dog, better than a bear. Better than a wolf, even, which I heard they're seeing up north. And pigs travel in packs too, like wolves; tusk instead of fang, swaggering, because no one can eat them now, not even a bear. Sometimes from Bio Sci you look down into the trees, see the big boars shivering the trunks with their bodies, like boats in the thick water, no wake at all from the sows and piglets. *When all the plants are dead*, we would ask in class, *what do they eat?* And our teachers never said. Later, we knew the answer was everything, anything. That's why they palisaded the campus at several points, Larsen told us. Because in the old days, in the cold, the boars came up, quietly, on cloven and padded hooves, and killed and ate. Chickens. Rabbits. Dogs, cats. The recently buried. The slow, the drunk, the unwary, the unlucky.

What was Nadiya's cat named again? My God. It is impossible that I have forgotten. Sleek and dainty, something about stars, not Star though, not Sky, not Stella. Galaxy? Nebula? The kind of black that looked blue in certain lights. We joked that she was part-magpie (though she never killed a magpie, that we saw; she never left the tenth floor).

Anyway. They said the world shifted suddenly — lurched, really — from big, slow-growing animals that ate a few things, like elephants and tigers, to smaller, faster ones that eat many things, like mice and sparrows; and I do not know which the wild pigs are, huge survivors or exceptions to some rule, but they do have an awful lot of piglets virtually year-round, so there is no time when you can really be safe. They are always defending babies. They are always defending carcasses. They are always angry to see you. And they are always a tremendous, tremendous amount of food. You get tired of plants. Protein always at a premium: an egg, once or twice a week. But this, this.

I am early; the big waterclock in quad to which we sync our individual wind-up clocks says five forty. But I could not risk staying in the house long enough to have Mom watch me try to nonchalantly leave, bristling with metal and glass like a porcupine. I sit at a bench under the huge dead trees and breathe the fog into myself, pretending that as I exhale something goes with it: the burning acid in my empty stomach, fear, adrenaline, something. Inside I want only pure water. It doesn't work.

Just as Henryk said, the platform is gone — folded up again and put away for the next time it's needed. I wonder if they washed, scraped, sanded the blood off. Or if they just left it, and the next time someone has to make a speech or something, they will have to stand on that redblack landscape.

It would be cleaner in the domes, I think again, unable to stop myself from imagining it. Whatever they did would be sterile. Fast. Or maybe they don't do this at all. Kill people. Maybe I will come back and say: We don't have to do this.

Henryk arrives next, of course; I had known he would. Maybe just in the general way that acknowledges that we are the only two who have never gone on a pig hunt, that we will be the youngest, the lightest, the weakest, the most likely to fuck up and be fucked up, and (as a result of all those things) the most scared. He too came here to breathe the pure water, I think. Breathe out the fear.

"I restrung my bow," he says, by way of greeting. "But then I didn't bring it. I was like: Well what the hell is an *arrow* going to do against an eight-hundred-pound pig?"

"Did people use to hunt those things with arrows? Back Then?"

"Maybe thrillseekers did. If they had crossbows. But honestly I mean, all that hair, right. All that fat. And then I don't think it was for food, because practically everybody bought their food in stores."

"Imagine *seeking out* a thrill and not even eating it. Jesus."

"Yeah."

I shift uncomfortably on the cold plastic, the dew soaking into my pants. "Do you remember the name of Nadiya's cat?"

"Cassiopeia."

"*That's* what it was. I was a mile off. That's right: for the beautiful queen who knew she was beautiful."

He laughs, but it's got kind of a nervous, cawing quality to it; I half-expect a crow to hop out of the mist to see who's calling. We've both got that fist of embers under our ribs: fear burning a hole. I tell myself it's excitement, it's anticipation, but it doesn't work. Can't just rename a thing and expect it to change what it's always been. Look at Cassiopeia, who acted like royalty when she was a flea-sick kitten.

"Look what came in the mail yesterday." Henryk pulls out an envelope of his own: pinkish paper flecked with black, laborious dark green writing. They've misspelled his name: *HENRY*, in widely spaced block letters. "From my uncle Dex. Dad's brother?"

"No kidding. The one that moved up north, right? Where the tar lakes are?"

"Yeah. I haven't seen him for a long time." He pushes the envelope back into his jacket. "He came a couple of months after the funeral."

I remember him now: tall, rangy, slow-moving, slow to speak, with a silver-shot black beard, no Cad. When we were introduced, he had shaken my hand with extraordinary delicacy, as if he were handling a sparrow's egg. An awkward stranger, grieving dutifully, friendly enough but obviously relieved that Hen wanted to stay here instead of leaving with him, his only surviving family. "How is he doing?"

"Good. He wants to know if I . . . if I want to come up and work with him."

A startled, silver flash of pre-emptive horror and loneliness before I remember that I am leaving too; either way, we are leaving one another, and I had let myself forget it in my eagerness to be gone. Selfish. Be happy for him, goddammit. He's happy for me, after all. I swallow, hard. "Work doing what?"

"He partnered up with a couple of Chip friends, and they have a tree farm and a big hothouse. He says they could use a body on the business end of things, and planting trees and looking after them till they're delivered. Says it's wetter up there. Cooler. Quiet. There's hunting, real good fishing."

"Mm. You gonna go?"

"I wrote back yesterday to say I would go check it out."

"If it doesn't work, you can always come back down."

"Yeah. That's what I said. But I'm excited to go." He stares out into the fog, still untenanted. Five minutes to six. "I've never been anywhere."

"Yeah."

"And it's, it's like . . . it's kind of like what you're doing. I mean much less, what's the word — prestigious, obviously," he says all in a rush, not looking at me; his hair hangs over his eyes, dripping. "But it feels right. Both of us trying to work with the — with the land. It's like, we can just live in this, or we can try to make things better. You know? It's not all about, it can't be all about just — walking along with your head down because that's what everybody else is doing. Everything in the whole world is waiting to be picked up and fixed. Not starting over. Starting from new."

"Hen, I think you're doing something even better than that. Because yeah, there *are* people working on what was left behind. But you, you're going to be making things that fix themselves — that fix more than just themselves too. Those baby trees won't fix things from Back Then, and that's good. Maybe . . . maybe none of that deserves to be fixed. Look at what it did to the people who made it. They broke the whole world with it."

"Yeah." He looks up at last, eyes glowing, pleased. His skin still has the greenish cast of fear. "Cool, right?"

"It'll be amazing. An adventure. Bigger and better than mine, because I'll be at school again."

"Two adventures. Yeah." Shadows begin to coalesce out of the mist, prickly, like me, with spears but also clubs and far more esoteric weapons, swathed in scarves and coats. "I mean. *If* we survive today and don't get eaten by a pig."

"I'll give a real good speech at your funeral, buddy."

"Me too."

"There might not be anything to bury."

"I know. I read they can crunch bones and everything. Their teeth can eat our teeth."

"Great." I want to turn and run; or I want to run towards the others and tell them I've changed my mind. Instead as the clock strikes its tinny tones, six on the dot, I stand, straighten up, walk.

There's Koda, swathed in pale leather; McKinnon, like a building moving through the fog, holding a spear I could not even get my hand around. I suppose they have planned it so that if a killing blow must be delivered, it will be by him. Good. We already know he is unmindful of pain, fear, and death.

The Dufresne twins have also been invited, Rene delineated with Cad like the black lines on a globe, Emil's skin flawless, gold-brown as the polished wood of the library, their neatly braided hair tied back so that not even one thin dark rope can move. Carefully looping his lasso, Rene nods only at me; Emil does not, instead slowly blinking, like a cat saying hello. They both carry their weight on the balls of their feet, light and confident.

Another face looks familiar, and I stare unabashedly until I can place it: Aldous Wong, who was a few grades ahead of Henryk and me, track star, poet, coveted by many romantic dreamers (in silence, fearful of his disdain), whose hair used to fall in a silky black curtain to the middle of his back. Now, it is cut so short I can see his scalp. He takes the same amount of time to recognize me, and lifts his chin in a gesture of greeting.

We all live on campus, I assume, but the circles people move in don't always intersect. And the other three I don't know at all. A foxy-looking man, a big blonde woman in light furs, a tall thin boy perhaps my age, wearing an ostentatious spiral-woven leather necklace with a single boar tusk dangling from it. Koda won't like that. Make him stick it under his shirt. You shouldn't have anything that could tangle or clink or catch, and not for vanity's sake especially. Wait a minute, do I know his face? Yes . . . the boy that came into the store a few days ago. The one with rabbit jerky to trade.

Koda says, "All right, here's the plan —" and glares when the foxy man cuts her off.

"Who're these two?"

"Extra eyes and beaters." She folds her broad arms across her chest in a gesture akin to a rooster fluffing up before a rival, though her tone is mild. "Problem with that, Kavanagh?"

"No'm," he says at once, though his darting eyes are still narrowed, the irises a pale, bilious green under gingery brows. He has no spears or knives, only a thick black PVC bow and a quiver. "No problem. Only, I didn't sign up to be no babysitter."

"Me either," says the tall boy, petulantly. "Hey, you two. You ever been on a boar hunt?"

"Pig hunt," I say. "No."

Henryk remains silent at my side, though there is a kind of shivery expectancy to him.

"Didn't think so. Fucking useless," the boy says. "Why'd you bring them?"

I want to *scream* at them. I need this! You don't need this like I need this! You're just doing this for the ... for the bragging rights, to show off to your friends!

If they say I can't go, I'll ... But the important thing is to hide my desperation, so I simply watch them, unmoving.

"I said I'd arrange for a hunt, and I arranged for it." Koda's voice remains level, emotionless; both Tusk Necklace and Kavanagh step back all the same. The blonde woman says nothing, though her face is lightly twisted with distaste. "I'll vouch for them both, Gabriel."

"I don't care. We don't need 'em and I don't want 'em."

Aldous startles me by speaking up, gliding forward so that his shoulder touches the boy Gabriel's. "I'll vouch for Reid. She was a fighter in school."

"No I wasn't."

"I didn't say a good one," he says placidly. "But she's not afraid to step in."

Emil lifts his lip to expose one canine, and spits onto the dust near my boot, kicking up an impressive little crater. "She's sick. She won't do what needs doing."

I'm startled by this too, and instinctively glance at Rene, who has worn a sleeveless fox-fur vest in what you might think was a deliberate choice to expose his own disease: thick ropes of colour flowing under his skin, tumorous in the darkness of rib-shadow. A single flicker of hate, even despair, passes across his face so rapidly that at first I believe I have imagined it. They have fought about this before, I suspect. Rene is here on his brother's suffering and imagined no other sufferers would be allowed to come. Now, we are two liabilities instead of one, and Emil is scared. And my fear worsens, seeing his.

But I'm scared of not being allowed to come with them too. Of forever thinking about the one in a million opportunity I would give up if I could not leave something behind in my place. Please, please. I don't have the time for anything else. I just don't.

"Beaters don't step in," Koda says. "It'll be fine."

"What about this one? Weedy boy. Look at him. Who will vouch for him?"

No one does. Even I cannot, under the unspoken rules of this engagement now begun. They seethe in silence when even Aldous does not speak. After a moment, Koda says, "Let's go. We're burning away the dawn."

"No!" Kavanagh strides too close to Koda; he is shorter than she, but is humming with anger now, righteously, it seems. "This is no game! Listen, we signed on for this with the understanding that you knew what you were doing, and if you're bringing on a couple of kids so young they're still shitting in their nappies, then that ain't the case, and you don't. You can count us out. Right? Gabe? Elle?"

The boy nods eagerly, the tusk jerking on his chest; the blonde woman — Elle — shrugs.

Kavanagh says, "Them or us."

Koda glances at me, at Henryk. Well, that's an easy choice, I think gloomily. Koda asked me out of pity, knowing that I needed this, and never expected Henryk to tag along. We are not needed here. They're right.

"All right," Koda says, and hefts her spear, already turning away. "Go organize your own hunt then. Everyone else: to me."

"Wait!"

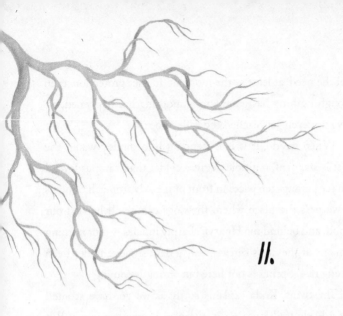

II.

Oh no, say my knees as we take the Drop stairs down into the valley, but their worry is for nothing — I guess the rapid ascent the other day wasn't as dire as they thought it was. We move in silence, with exaggerated care to not slide or stumble. A few feet in front of me, Elle gives off a pleasant, musky smell, like the secret inner bark of a pine tree. I wonder what a pig would think of it. Something good, I decide; she is covered in furs, and if she is wearing those on a hunt she must have dozens more, so she's good at this, she knows how animals think, smell, move, die.

Kavanagh, stomping as we left campus, has pushed the anger out of his muscles now, and moves with soundless ease; even the tall boy, Gabriel, who looked so gangly and clumsy, seems to float. McKinnon is our loudest member, but there's nothing we can do about that. The Dufresnes and Aldous stick together, and I walk with Henryk and Koda. Uneasily, I feel the need, at least at the moment, for her protection, even though nothing has gone wrong, nothing has happened, we have not even yet reached the valley floor.

When we do, it is like stepping into muddy water; the mist is stagnant, multiple degrees colder than campus level. I can see perhaps ten paces in front of me. My stomach tightens as we pass the place where the dogs came and harried our rabbit, and behind me Henryk sharply inhales — but nothing remains of the dog's carcass, only a dark smudge under fresh green grass. Spring is not here but spring is coming.

The twins, Koda explains softly as we go, have scouted out a likely trail; once on it, the plan is simple enough. But everyone needs to know their place. If you are where you are not supposed to be, you will be subject to friendly fire, and there will be no quarter, because there will be no time. The pigs are big but quick, far quicker than you would expect if you have never encountered them in a tight spot, and of course Henryk and I have not. We will need them to be in a tight spot and us not to be, and the slope and the underbrush are no help to us; the only way we fence them in is with our bodies. And that is what Henryk and I have been brought along to do.

Aldous whispers: "Bait. Wait. Aggravate." I laugh nervously under my breath, and appreciate the minimal turn of his head, the edge of his smile. One dimple. I am terrified, but I can remember three words. How many of these hunts has he been on? You hardly ever hear about them. Or, that is to say, you hear about them when people return with carcasses. Maybe the ones that fail we just never hear about.

I think of Bashir climbing his stepladder, writing my name, Henryk's name, on the board in the store. All those names. Columns and columns and columns, every week. And nothing in births. Hardly ever. The opposite, I think resentfully, of the pigs, who have piglets every year and hardly ever die; why, those who have never seen a hunt must think they're nigh immortal. Unfair.

(But nothing is fair. Nothing is fair.)

By the time we reach the scouted spot in the thick of the valley, the mist has mostly burned away; scraps remain at ankle-level, golden in the early sun. My fear too has mostly burned off. Nothing will happen, it says. It surges back with an almost audible yell when we see the tracks in the mud, instantly recognizable, far bigger than I had expected, even with Koda's warnings. Oh God. Oh God. And farther up the path: bigger still. A mixed group with some real monsters in it.

Pack of demons. Sulphur breath. Cloven as the devil. Calm down, quick: the invader in me cannot see what is happening, it only knows to respond to my fear. Can't risk it acting up. We haven't even glimpsed a pig yet.

I take several deep breaths, and help the others heap the bait. Don't want it too spread out. Cooked potatoes, raw turnips and rutabagas, a few mealy apples that Emil, unnecessarily, stomps to release their juices. *Pigs like the night*, Koda said on the way down. *So now they should be on their way back to sleep. That will be our chance.*

This is how we kill, I think, as we move into position. We wait until things are weak and tired, and we pick off the garbage, skinny, glaze-eyed unlucky beasts. How different from Back Then, when everyone was as strong and splendid as gods. Meat and milk and sugar every day. Replete with iron and calcium, shiny-eyed, clean-skinned, and Cad still sleeping wherever it was it slept. (But did it sleep? What were you before you could control us? Did you live in the earth, listening, waiting for a day? Did you swim in the wine-dark sea?)

We kill with shame now, because we have to. And then we are humiliated even as we bring back our prizes. Not trophies, like the old days, mounted on the walls in the Agriculture building — sawdust-stuffed, crawling with bugs, ancient horns. We eat the head. No sense wasting the meat and the brawn.

I have to get out of this place.

(I can't)

(I know)

Koda places me upslope between Rene and Henryk, then arranges Aldous, Gabriel, and Emil into a not-quite-closed circle; she stands at the open end with the others. When the pigs arrive, we must herd them by whatever means necessary into a tight group to send them straight towards the hunters, no detours. The hunters will deliver a minimum number of killer blows with support from Emil's lasso to tangle and create obstructions with fallen giants. "If all goes well," Koda whispers, "everything will be over in a minute or two."

We just have to keep the circle intact. Move as one. Watch where the others are, and do not let the circle be broken.

The long spear is unfamiliar but light in my trembling grip. I loosen the straps on the two short ones so I can quickly grab them if I use

(drop)

this one. Shut up! I tell my fear. You're not helping.

I think of old illustrations in our books: bullfighters in colourful capes, the big animal bristling with small insults just sharp enough to stick in its skin. If you stabbed me, I'd burst into tears and curl into a ball, I think; not run at you with my horns. Different strokes, I guess. They teach you these things from history and say, *Maybe you can apply this to your everyday life*, and we just scoff, don't we? Nothing from Back Then applies, till suddenly it does. Anyway, my blade is sharp, and more importantly is metal rather than glass, so it will not break. And if I get in a good stab, I suppose even if I don't kill the pig, it'll get tetanus later. Take that.

I hold down a giggle and glance at Henryk, who is paler than I've ever seen him, as if he might vomit, that peculiar colour of grey with two red dots right underneath his eyes. Even his hair seems leached of colour: like old straw instead of its usual brown. Aldous looks a lot better, alert and erect, a short spear lying along either forearm. He catches my eye and raises an eyebrow, not quite a smile but a "You all right?" shorthand. I don't think so, but I raise mine back.

Koda has chosen well. It's barely a half hour before the first pigs arrive, walking slowly and without fear in their own footsteps. I am as stunned as if I'd seen dinosaurs. Be casual, I tell myself, but I have only ever seen them in drawings and photographs, and most of those have been of domestic pigs before they began to interbreed with the imported wild boar. Clean and pink in their pens, or smug, half-submerged in mud in kids' books. Piggies going to market, jiggety-jig.

These are not those pigs. They are wolfish, they strut and sneer; their hair is like the barbed wire of the palisades, forest camouflage of grey, black, and brown. They don't have tusks, it seems at first, and I almost let myself relax: you can still get run down, of course, but you won't get gored to death or —

— oh. No. Because here come the big boars, and they *do* have tusks, and they shout directly at my lizard brain, telling me to run, a predator is too near, there are only two of them but I am staring at their tusks, as long as my bent arms, with broken edges sharper than a surgeon's chisel, virulently dirty. Their shoulders are the same height as mine.

I had pictured them shrunken and winter-wan, like the hare we caught. In no pocket of my imagination existed these monsters. At their feet run the only things that you might be able, I feel, to kill: piglets of numerous ages, busy under the protective shadows of their elders.

As one, they see the bait. There is a clumsy but urgent stampede; I freeze, try to push some blood into my frozen legs, and see Koda shaking her head minutely: Not yet. All right. Let them get stuck in. We are far enough up the slope that they would have to crane their necks to look at us, and that seems to be a motion that they cannot do. What they will do, though, is hear us if we move, so we must wait. Concentrate, I tell myself, on not producing any *smells*.

The pigs are bunched together, the two big boars on opposite sides. I think of old men glaring at one another in the Dining Hall over grudges hatched sixty years ago, refusing to share a table. Choice morsels drop from the pigs' rapidly moving jaws, the piglets beneath darting in and out to scavenge. Silence. Wind moving through branches, the slightest swelling of buds. You have to trust that they will burst into green soon. You have to trust that the dark dead will bloom into life. Because right now your eyes tell you that nothing is coming. And the pigs think: We wait on leaves, and now, here is food. Strange.

Koda brings her hand down.

For a split second, none of us moves. Then Rene bounds down the slope, and I leap after him, using the butt of my spear as a third leg, trying to keep the trap intact like we were told. From the corner of my eye I see Aldous and Emil take off, Gabriel's shiny head moving above them all, adjusting to their pace.

It's not till we're down and shouting at the pigs and slapping the branches that I realize there's a gap: Henryk. And by then it's too late.

We're yelling, the pigs shrieking and stomping ahead of us, spinning, and in their spinning seeing two gaps, one containing three heavily armed humans, and one containing only the thawing forest and their own familiar footprints.

The babies break first, vanishing with terrified squeals. "You son of a bitch!" someone shouts, at Henryk, I think, who I can't even see. Did he run back up the hill? Faint? Is he lying in the dead grass? "You son of a bitch!" It's Gabriel, upset, not angry I now see but frightened, as the rest of the pigs spot the gap and bolt after their young.

"Close up!" Aldous yells, and Rene and I barrel towards the pigs coming our way, hoping they will see the gap vanish. They must, *must* reverse towards the hunters: Elle and Koda, McKinnon and his pig-sticking spear. "Close! Turn them! Quick!"

The herd screeches to a halt as we flail our spears at them, digging their hooves into the churned dust and leaves; Rene is coughing, unable to catch his breath, the tips of his spears waving wildly back and forth. The pigs scream as he jabs at them, they back up, and for a moment I think we've done it, we're doing it, we're back on the plan, they'll run towards death.

Then he falls, and one of the big sows barrels towards the opening, blocked by nothing more than his supine body.

"Back, back, yah!" Waving a spear behind me, I run to Rene, his brother shouting along with me, the rope whirling through the air, slapping water from the branches above us. How blue the sky is, how black the traceries of limbs.

My spear connects with hair and hide, so hard I am sure for a second that I have broken my wrist, pain shooting up to my shoulder; I switch hands and thrust at their faces, seeking to steer them, not to kill. I hope they know that. I want to explain it. A blur of thundering legs, the stench of their bodies, pigshit, blood, dust.

"These two! These two! Let the rest go!"

I can't tell who's screaming. A man, anyway. Henryk's is the only voice I would know. Which two?

But Emil knows, and circles at once, the thick plastic rope weighted with stones whipping around his head, dust rising, falling. The released pigs thunder past, buffeting but not targeting me, and I almost allow myself to feel a moment's relief . . . until Rene begins to rise, teeth gritted, mouth full of blood, fighting what, I don't know — the dust, the fear, his disease — and one of the big boars, shockingly, inevitably, pivots and heads for him.

"Reid!" Aldous, gripping his spear and thrower. I am horrified to see a black arrow sprouting from his shoulder, more than a foot long. He moves as if it is not there. "Get out of the way!"

Emil is running for his brother just behind Aldous, the rope loose now, coming to kill, thinking only of the fallen. "Get down!"

The boar hits all three of them.

Screaming, cracking. In the commotion I cannot even see faces, only that a slender body is flung into the trees, and then something knocks me flat with sickening speed. I crash into the brush, instinctively rolling into a ball, covering my face. Something closes around my ankle, hot and wet, and then I am tossed back into the light, time slowing down just as it did before. Just as when I

(it)

saw the dogs.

They were right. Right. The disease. Everything in me, every muscle, every nerve, wants me to curl up and play dead. I cannot reach for my spears. A sow has my leg in its mouth; in a second she will bite down, as she should, because I threatened the babies, and if bloodloss does not kill me today, blood poisoning will kill me within the week.

And I left no true will. No love note for my mother. Only the heap of yarn scavenged from the garbage of the old world. Only that.

"Reid!" A pleading note in the fluted treble. I am the closest to Aldous and Rene now, I think, and the boar is vulnerable, distracted, but I can't, I can't move, I am trapped and aside from that, I am trapped, doubly trapped, paralyzed from within. I'm sorry, I want to scream back. But it won't let even my lips move. *Stay silent*, it says. *Stay alive.*

No! Let me go!

Kavanagh soars out of nowhere, screaming at a pitch so high that I can only hear the barest edge of it, and looses three arrows into the sow as quickly as I could shoot one. His arms are a blur, reaching back, nocking, drawing, releasing.

And something within me pauses in astonishment, watching this, and that gives me the chance, a split second before it notices again, to jerk my ankle free and snatch at my bound spears — one, two. It takes me a while to rejoin the others, collapsing into the dust at first on a leg that will not hold me.

Not broken, I tell myself. Not broken, don't you dare be broken. It is not, and I'm up again and running back towards the dust and the heavy milling shapes, and someone is at my side — Emil, grim-faced and bloodied. At the last moment he closes his hands around the spear I hold, throws his weight behind it at the same moment I do, easily, effortlessly, like a dance, and we slam into a hairy thrashing side like a ton of bricks.

Things gallop past us and vanish. I collapse next to the carcass with my spear sticking out of it, and something razor-edged seems to catch in my throat — the dust becomes a glass-edged burr, and I cough and cough without budging the obstacle, it only becomes sharper and larger till my stomach convulses and I spit a few mouthfuls of vomit, and then at last the coughing stops. Everything dims for a moment, gradually returns to blue light. Emil lies at my side, facedown. I nudge him with my boot till he wearily rises.

Blood gleams in the little pool of puke I left behind. I look at it just long enough to confirm what I'm seeing, and then walk back to the others.

We have taken three pigs — the sow studded with Kavanagh's arrows, the boar Emil and I speared, and an enormous sow with no fewer than *ten* spears sticking out of it. I can barely bring myself to approach our boar, even though it is dead. Its gaping mouth is filled with blood, the tongue indistinguishable in the red. White bone gleams where a spear-thrust glanced off and only flensed it instead of penetrating.

The pigs, too, have taken three.

Gabriel lies clearly dead, his skull trampled into pulp, torso gored in stripes of unbelievable violence and depth, as if someone had gone at him not with a blade but an auger. His tusk necklace on its tough leather is intact though, and sparkles with obscene purity on what remains of his chest.

Rene Dufresne too has been run through and run over, unconscious, though he is still breathing, a ragged, bubbly sound. I am terrified that the third body facedown in the mud will be Henryk, but it is Aldous, moaning low and constant. Elle makes to roll him out of the dust, at least take the weight off the arrow that is slowly working its way through his shoulder, and Koda barks for her to stop: his back is broken.

Jesus. Jesus fuck.

At last something sinks in through the shock, something descending through tainted water. Aldous, our fastest hunter. At school so fast he seemed to lift off and fly around the track, leaving the other kids behind panting, pitifully earthbound. His hair streaming behind him shiny as a flag. Caught at last, by pigs. Of all things. Because of our incompetence and plain bad luck.

Someone is tugging at my coat; I turn in anger, because if it is Henryk, I swear to God — but it is Koda, weary, I think unhurt, two tear tracks slicing dramatically down her cheeks through the dirt. She is pushing something into my hand. I look down, and jump as something looks back at me: watery brown-red eyes surrounded by inky curls, a cut in the eyebrow drooling fresh blood. A mirror. My face.

"Can you climb?" Koda says hoarsely, gesturing at one of the dead poplars near the killing ground.

No, I want to say. Probably not.

But I take it, and I try. And just as in the church, the invader fights me, trying various strategies — pulling me back to the ground, curling my hands into fists, giving me vertigo, even darkening my vision — but as it pauses to reassess each effort, inch by inch I snarl and snap and make it up the tree, and sit in the crotch of a branch, flashing Koda's message to the station across the river, calling for help, asking them to amplify back to the station at campus. No mention is made of success.

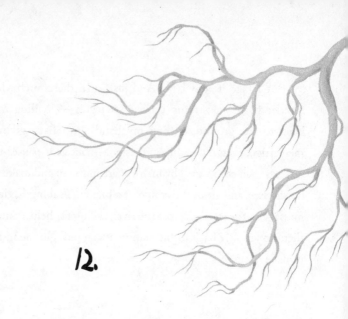

12.

As is tradition, Gabriel's share of the meat is offered to his survivors — his wife and father. Both decline, so as is also tradition it is given to the Dining Hall. The rest of us keep ours. From three pigs it is an impossible weight; Koda sends a runner with a soap-smelling note bearing the exact amount on it in pounds and kilograms, and her stamp as the pledge, while I am in the hospital getting washed up and stitched closed. I carefully put the note in my pocket so that I do not disturb this process. Dr. Gagliardi does not like the sow bite on my ankle, which broke the skin.

"I don't like it either," I point out.

"You, don't talk." She growls faintly as she sews, and I stare at the wall; I think watching her sew me up would be one thing, but I cannot for some reason stand to look at a curved needle doing so. There is a faded poster behind sun-yellowed plastic that details all the parts of the ear and the inside of the nose, which is at least something to read.

She mutters, "Goddamn kid. What were you thinking, going on this? Why am I wasting thread on someone so fucking stupid? This is gonna go bad. Guarantee it. You could lose your leg."

She does not add: I mean to say your life. You only have so much blood in you.

I know, I want to reassure her.

I try to feel terror about the impending ordeal — the creeping gangrene, the pus, the stench, the fever, and then those frenzied minutes on the operating table, strapped down and screaming around the gag — but it all feels incredibly far away. Maybe I did not deserve to be admitted to Howse, and maybe I did not deserve to be invited to go on the hunt, but Dr. G is right about one thing I do deserve: to die for it.

The leg is nothing. You can get by fine with a non-whole number of legs. There should be a more sinister punishment for being a murderer. And there is. The gallows only just taken down. They should have kept it up.

True, I do not know how much of the death and disaster down there was my fault through inaction or action. How much was simply the well-oiled machine of the other hunters working around two scared and inexperienced kids. How much was the Cad. How much was my fear. How much was luck, wind direction, phase of the moon. I don't know, but I feel certain, I feel surety, in my gut, in my bones, that none of this would have happened if I hadn't come. And if it is the disease making me so certain, if it is making me think this and be unable to tell that it's not me thinking it, I should die. I can't live with something in there insinuating itself into my thoughts in a way that I cannot flag. It should know that.

A lot of people with Cad do die by suicide, of course. It's all up there on the board. It's considered a natural cause of death if you have Cad. It is barely considered death in fact, only the silent withdrawal of a token future.

Listen. A long time ago, the people of Back Then put people on the moon; and later, they put people on Mars. Just a handful, fired there on ultrafast graphene-silver quantum torus engines. Twelve astronauts, American and Russian and Japanese and Chinese, and they inflated a shiny white hexagonal building, and they drove around exploring and taking samples and measurements, and they answered questions for schoolkids in video chat, and they recorded thousands of hours of their daily lives, and then one day they asked, "When is the next supply ship arriving?" and instead of a date the answer was "We'll get it to you, don't worry."

Because the world was on fire. The whole world was on fire and starving and at war, and no one could launch anything. And one day the astronauts opened up their video chat and said, "There are still supplies left, but we do not want you to watch what happens next," and they turned off all their communications.

I don't know why I'm thinking about that. Maybe it's the Cad again. *Go somewhere dark*, it says. *Secret.* Or I'm saying it. I don't know. *Go somewhere dark and secret, and die.* It is not unjust, untimely, not a tragedy, it is not *bad*. It is natural and good. Cats do it. Dogs do it. Have to look in dark closets and hidden cabinets when someone's sick pet disappears.

Dr. G finishes, washes her hands again, washes my foot, swathes it in bandages, pins them savagely on, still muttering to herself. The grey in her hair is a galaxy. The whole Milky Way, distracting me from the throb. The rest of my cuts she declares trifling, though they are full of forest debris and need a lot of scrubbing to clean out. "They'll scab," she says shortly. "Get out of here. I'll see you again tomorrow to look at that bite. Go talk to reception about times."

Outside, I bump into Emil, dazed-looking, scratched and scabbed all over, bleeding slowly onto the floor through the bandages the medics hastily wrapped down in the valley. There are chairs, but he leans against the wall as if it makes a difference. An enormous rope burn around his arm is so raw and weepy that I flinch to look at it. His sleeves hang in tatters.

I nod to him, but he stops me as I walk past, his hand on my wrist tight and hot so that I look up at him, immediately fearful. He's lost a tooth: that lovely white canine. His lip is split below it, black and plump. "Where is the boy."

"What?"

"The boy you came with," he says slowly, his gaze not leaving mine. "The one who broke the circle. Him."

"I don't know."

He squeezes my wrist, hard, but it is the work of a moment to twist it towards him and so free myself. But I don't step back. Fucking touch me again. Try it. We are just about nose to nose, breathing each other's rank and rotten breath, full of bile, dead adrenaline, swallowed blood.

"You know him," he says. "I've seen you with him. I know I have. Where is he. Where does he live."

"Enough. You stay the fuck away from him."

Big words, as I limp away, stiff with pain and pride. Big words. Because I want to fucking kill Henryk too.

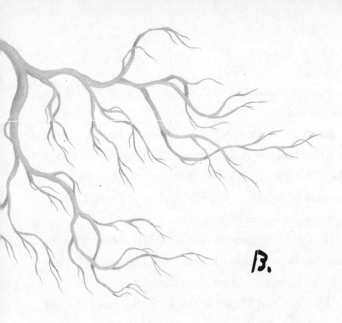

13.

When I finally find him, hidden in the basement of the Chemistry building, my anger has dissipated; because I know he wanted to be found. He hid here knowing that *I* would find him. In silence, shamed, he evades my gaze, and nods meekly when I suggest we go outside.

The crowds of people that would normally be congratulating the boar hunters, singing the songs of celebration, negotiating to buy or beg meat to smoke for the Farrowfair, never materialized. No one sang a single note for us, even when the three huge bodies were displayed in the open of the quad. Now that, *that* they should have left the platform up for. Undeniable murderers. Not alleged. Justice in some way served by letting people see the carcasses.

That had been hours ago. I had gone to find my mother, dragging myself up and up the endless steps, but she had not been there, and Yash and Maliah were gone too. No one spoke to me.

Henryk saw her, though. We sit on the cement steps of the Chem building in the gathering dusk; I am lightheaded, I have not eaten even one bite from my hundreds and hundreds of pounds of kill. It's good to sit down. I stretch my bandaged leg out in front of me.

He says, "She came to my office. Said she went to the soapworks to look for you, but she didn't find you. Hours ago. And then someone told her about the hunt."

"You. You told her about the hunt, you mean. Because you can't keep your fucking mouth shut about anything. Anything in the whole world."

He curls in on himself, a spider in a flame, arms going around his knees, face burying in his thighs. No reply. When I first found him he was folded up like this: as if I were going to kick him across the room. His face bright red and splotchy from crying.

"She didn't go back to our place after that. And Yash and Mal are gone too. I don't even know if they're together."

"I'm sorry."

"Gabriel is dead," I say after a long time. A magpie hops on the steps in front of us, hopefully, only its white parts visible. People must eat here. Toss it scraps. "The boy with the tusk necklace. He was married. Aldous has a broken back. And Rene Dufresne is in a coma. They're saying he might never wake up. Skull fracture."

He raises his face, wet with fresh tears. "It's all my fault.

I . . . I don't know. I was standing there. With my spear. Watching the rest of you. And all of a sudden, I was running, trying to be quiet . . . it was like something in a dream. Where you have to escape something big, but you're small, and you know you can find somewhere to hide that it won't see you. I wasn't even thinking. Not until I was halfway up the Drop, and I heard everybody screaming behind me, the pigs screaming, you all screaming. And I knew I couldn't come back down. I kept going. Came here. It's all my fault. I'm sorry. I'm so sorry."

"I froze. Me and Rene both did. It's our fault too."

"It's not your fault."

"Look," I say, gritting my teeth, "please shut the fuck up for just a minute. You weren't there. You don't know what happened."

He snuffles into his sleeve and clutches himself, shivering on the cold steps. I can't believe he volunteered to come. Just like that. Knowing that it might end like this: that it was more likely than not to end like this. He's the smart one, supposedly, out of the two of us. I can't believe I ever thought he was my anchor to anything, anything, knowing that he would look at me in danger, and drop his weapons and run lightly away so that no one would hear him. Even now, his sobs are strangely distant. Background noise. Like the hum of a crowd.

I have asked him to shut up but I know he can't, and he says thickly, half-choking, "Are we still friends? I don't blame you if you don't want to be friends any more."

But I'm holding myself too, my numb hands fastened onto opposite sides of my jacket, looking up at the last of the sunset: bruise-purple, blood-black, stars coming out. My stomach hurts. Dr. G, upon hearing about the blood in my vomit, told me that I likely had some internal bleeding, but for that, there was nothing she could do. It would have to heal or not on its own.

The magpie gives up on us and hops off, not even deigning to fly. I don't even know, really, why I went looking for Henryk. Part of me wanted to beat him up. Part of me just wanted to know what happened: Had he been hurt? Had he been sick? No. Just a coward.

Cowardice: I can leave that behind. I can give that up.

He's the one always saying that it's too late to start over; and I agree now, I see what he means. He means the world, but it applies to everything. It's always too late. It's never in time. But there's always time to start afresh, point a different way, do something else, make something new. The end of the world makes a clean slate to build a new one.

I get up slowly from the steps and walk home, and I don't look back to see if he's following me.

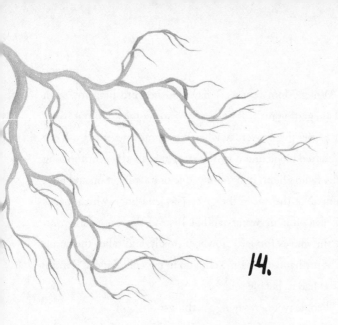

14.

Mom doesn't come home until the next evening, when I have quietly made as many inquiries as I think I can make without letting people know how crazed I am with worry, just short of getting her name up on the board. Even Larsen looks at me blankly, and says, very casually, that she'll poke around.

She does not congratulate me on the boar hunt. As I leave, I find myself wobbly-legged with relief that she has not.

Our place seems too big and too quiet. Never used to solitude, never used to not hearing another voice on the far side of the wall, feeling the air move with someone's breath. This, this aching void, this is what I would leave her with. This is what she fears. Well, you get used to it, I suppose. When people die, when people sicken . . . but to have someone leave you, to hand this void to you and expect you to take it. That is what hurts her. I get it now.

When Mom returns, I have finished brushing my teeth and am getting ready for bed, trying to get the knots out of my hair. Easier than yesterday, when it took me forever to wash out the clotted blood and dirt. We stare at each other for too long in the fading light. In a minute, one of us will get up and light a lamp. Not the one in the green jam jar, I hope, which makes us look a bit underwatery and ill. Instead, the room darkens.

She moves forward slowly, formally, and takes the comb out of my hand, tilting my chin up in her cold fingers. "Hmm. Not as bad as people said."

"People were . . . saying . . . things?"

"They said your face was completely ruined," she says. "It's just the one big cut here, and that'll heal clean. And some scratches."

She sits on the bed, and I turn on my chair and look at her; our faces are almost on the same level when we sit like this. My heart pounds so that I think I might be sick. "I did it for you. Giving you my share. So that when I go . . ."

"That's what Henryk said." Her voice is flat, noncommittal; it tells me nothing. It takes me several moments to realize just how incandescently angry she is.

"It's a lot. Look." I give her Koda's note, but she doesn't bother unfolding it, only sits very still, back straight, with the paper shaking in her hands. Thunderheads cluster in the room. I wait for them to break.

"Reid, you're not ready for this. Ready to go to university. Or live on your own. This just cements it: this is proof, everyone I've talked to agrees with me."

"Who were you t—"

"Don't interrupt me. This was the decision of a child — trying to buy your way into something, as if throwing away your life to hunt a dangerous animal would prove that you were ready to travel thousands of miles by yourself for something that might not even exist. And you're sick, you know that, and you still went. And look what happened. Gabriel Bramswell is dead."

"Mom, I didn't have anything to do with that. I don't know what people were telling you, or who . . . who *did* you talk to? Who told you what happened down there? Don't say Henryk."

"Why would Henryk know wh— . . . oh Reid, for God's sake. For fuck's sake."

I have never heard her swear before; it is like being slapped. Tears rise to my eyes, first one, then the other, and begin to burn down my cheeks like molten tar.

"Did you take him along with you on that — on that suicide mission? Did you drag him along?"

"No! He volunteered to go! He wanted to go!"

"How can you look at me and lie like that? How? When you were a little girl — no, look at me — when you were a little girl, remember, we sat down and had that talk, about how you wouldn't lie to me, and I wouldn't lie to you, because it was just the two of us —"

I'm weeping now. How dare she. The two of us: an open wound. Just the two of us now. I don't remember that, only that it was winter, and we had birch candy after, a tiny bite, *just for the children* (the sign said) but I had saved some of mine for her and even a little for Daddy, because she could not convince me he was not coming back. "I'm still going. I'm sorry I went on the hunt, because yeah, it was stupid, people got hurt, but I'm sorry, I'm still going."

"Is this the part where you tell me that I have to let you live your life?" At last she raises her voice, so that I can hear her over my sobs. Thoughtful of her. "Hmm? Is that what you're going to say?"

"No. Yes! Yes! I am saying that!"

"Because what do you think you're living now? What do you think this is? Not good enough for you? It's more real than anything in that letter could possibly be. You know — Reid, stop it this minute. You know Mrs. Cross doesn't do anything with those applications. She just wants you to write essays. I could go down to her office right now —"

"No!"

"— and find the stacks and stacks of them in the drawers, because she won't give them up to be recycled —"

"That's not true! She did send it away! They talked about my essay in the letter! They said that was why they were accepting me!"

"Reid, stop acting like a child. We can put this all behind us if you'll just calm down and be reasonable. I want to put it behind us. That's all I want."

"You want to put *everything* behind us! That's what you want! You don't want me to have a chance at something different and new, you're terrified of it, or your — your fucking disease is terrified of it, and one of you is saying this shit, and I can't tell the difference anymore! I can't tell the difference! I don't even know who I'm leaving!"

"You can just leave the Cad out of this," she hisses, standing, and I stand too, and I realize that I am taller than she is, which shouldn't be possible. "It doesn't factor into this at all. It's just an infection. It doesn't —"

"It does and you know it!" My tears dry and pull on my skin; I feel lit-up from inside, possessor of great and terrible secrets, iron-hard, that I could pound into a spearpoint. "You think I'm grateful for the so-called benefits of this thing, you think that's it, don't you? That it keeps us out of trouble, keeps us safe. Well, *fuck* the benefits, and *fuck* Cad, fucking *parasite*!"

"You watch your language!"

"I didn't consent to having this thing in me!" I scream at last, even though the disease itself, as if to prove my point, flares, hurtful, in fingers and toes; it must be swirling angrily across my face like a dust devil. Mom is staring at my cheeks rather than my eyes, stunned.

"You don't consent to your genes either! That's an extremely childish argument, and you're going to need to lower your voice."

"It made Dad leave! That, that thing, inside you! That's what drove him off!"

Her eyes widen. Had I thought no more lines could be crossed? She strokes both hands through her hair and composes herself. "It had nothing to do with it. That was a decision he made on his own. How dare you suggest that —"

"It was the thing's fault!"

"That thing is part of you! And at least he came to visit your grandmother in the hospital! You didn't even see her — you didn't see your own grandmother, my mother, while she was dying!"

"Dying of this! Grandma was screaming, she was screaming while she died and there was nothing they could do, and you wanted me to talk to her like that, a five-year-old, you wanted a five-year-old child to hear her grandmother in the worst pain of her entire life, and you're a monster for that, you're a monster, and you're carrying a monster, and you made me a monster too, and I hate you for it! I hate you for *all of it*!"

Her face dissolves. Through a blue-tinted fog, I fling the comb at my desk, and then I am gone, hurling myself in bare feet down the slick concrete steps, something in me

(you know its name)

making me grasp the handrail to slow my headlong flight.

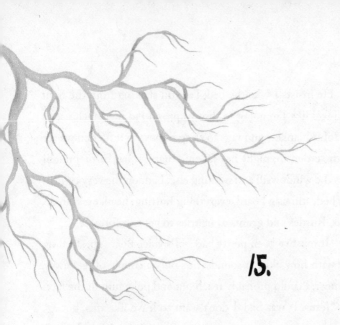

/5.

Henryk's door is shut, which causes me to goggle at it as if I've forgotten they could do that, which honestly I think I might have; it is so rare to see it done. But he opens it to my tap and lets me in, and I shut it again behind me because he seems to want it shut.

He is sleepy, damp, baffled, clearly about to turn in. I also get the impression that he somehow never expected to see me again. But I could not think of anywhere else to go, nowhere safe seemed safe enough, enough of a structure to protect me from my self-inflicted storm.

"Were you . . . crying?" he says cautiously.

"I had a fight with my mom."

"Oh. Um —"

"Can I sleep over? Just for tonight." I sniff, and rub a hand over my eyes.

"Of course."

He insists I take the bed; I'm still shaking from the fight and feel like I'm going to throw up, and I'm not much use as he folds blankets and rags to sleep in next to it. When we are both settled in, night has fallen; a narrow bar of moonlight hits the windowsill and nothing else. I am on the very edge of his bed, stiff as a board, everything hurting: head, eyes, ankle, guts. Rustles and grunts as he tries to get comfortable.

"It must've been pretty bad." His voice floats up, startling me with how close it sounds: he's only a couple of feet away, at most. I could probably reach out and poke him in the face.

"Jesus. It was bad. I don't want to leave like this, but . . . I don't see how I can stay after . . . after all the things I said."

"I don't want to go either," he says. "And I don't want you to go. But what are we supposed to do? Sometimes you can't . . . you can't build something new while you're standing in the spot where the old one is. You have to move. Build it from somewhere else."

"I guess." I'm stuffed up and can't breathe except through my mouth; annoyed, I roll onto my back and look up at the darkened ceiling, where a tiny mobile hangs, white paper cranes. Something his dad made, I think. "God. I'm such a . . . I'm such a terrible fucking everything. Daughter. Hunter. Friend. Maybe I can be a semi-decent student, I don't know. I hope they're not expecting miracles from me when I show up."

Silence. Murmurs from other walls. Finally Henryk says, "When Mom and Dad died? I thought I should die too. I didn't understand how it was possible that I had gotten sick and then gotten better, and that they had died. I started thinking of how I could die too. How to do it. You were the one who got me through that. No one else even really talked to me after the funeral."

"I remember that. Wait. You were going to kill yourself? You never said that."

"I didn't want you to talk me out of it."

"You bastard son of a bitch. I would have, too. I would have tied you to a chair and put you on a twenty-four-hour watch."

He laughs weakly. "I know. But you didn't need to save my life that way. You saved it anyway. You're not a bad friend. You're the best. You're good and smart and generous, and if you hadn't given so much of yourself to me in those six months, there would be nothing inside me at all except the black hole from where they died."

" . . . Well I don't think that's true. There's plenty inside you."

"Including you."

"I'm nothing much," I tell him, trying not to raise my voice. "I just said that."

"That's not true. You know? It's like clouds. They don't look like much. They look weightless, but they weigh millions and millions of tons."

"Bullshit. They're fluff. Like steam."

"No, they're not. Water is heavy. You can't tell from looking how much of a big deal something is."

"But —"

"I read about it. I'm not lying. Can you trust me, Reid? Can you trust me on this?"

I'm crying again, silently, tears leaking onto the pillow. I dab at them with the blanket. "Come up on the bed. It must be freezing down there."

He clambers awkwardly over me to the space between my back and the wall, all elbows and knees for a second; warmth blooms between as soon as we wrestle the blanket into place. We've never shared a bed before.

This is it, I guess; I said it, and he did it, and now I suppose we'll have to carefully, because I'm hurt, very carefully curl into each other, confess secret things, learn how to kiss; I am already imagining how strange the first one will be, not that I want him to, or do I? I'm not sure. It feels inevitable somehow. That he will slide his arms around me, that we will in our grief and our long-repressed (was it?) mutual lust finally let ourselves go, make love, not worry about protection so that I can carry his baby to university (wait: no, the timing's not right, maybe next week there would be a baby), no parents, no guilt, no shame. That this is the moment we both finally realize we've always been meant to be together: that anyone else didn't mean anything real.

I wonder if he can feel how fast my heart is beating, conducted through the wood of the bed. And then I realize, almost laughing, that he's simply pushed his face between my shoulderblades and gone to sleep.

Well, all right. Serves me right, too. Can you imagine. The embarrassment of it all.

Later, I wonder why I was waiting for him to make a move instead of making one myself, and then as I wonder this I realize I have woken up, and what's woken me up is my bladder. I eel off the bed, and hesitate. Bathrooms are down the hall, the only closed doors to keep in the smell before everything gets collected in the morning. I don't want to walk all the way down there in the dark. Chamber pot: where?

I fumble to his desk, where I remember seeing a lantern, and strike it into life, squeezing the shutter nearly closed, so that only a thin ray remains. Dozens of small oblongs on the floor — mousetraps. I'll have to watch my toes. He didn't have these last time I was in here, but now that I come to think of it, when am I ever in here? We're always at mine. Being mothered. Oh, Hen.

There's the chamberpot, on the floor next to the desk, and a stack of clean rags next to it in a basket. After I'm done, I realize that the "sweat" trickling down my face, in the chilly room, is blood; I press another rag to my eyebrow, and run my hand lightly over the top of the desk, looking for something that might serve as a mirror. He's not vain enough to have one like mine, maybe, but you can always check your reflection in something. There: glass. I pick up the bottle and inspect my face in it: yes, a scab has pulled off and dangles by a thread. Gross. I pick it off, toss it in the chamberpot, and firmly fit the rag to my brow again, sitting on the edge of the desk.

It is not till I'm about to shut off the lantern and return to bed, shivering, that I realize what I picked up. I glance back at Henryk: asleep, or at least unmoving, even though I threw the corner of the blanket over his face when I got up.

Then I heft the bottle again and hold it close to the lantern. It is not black as I had initially thought, but dark green. Ink. And the top drawer of the desk contains a few sheets of pink paper, speckled with black. I close it quietly, snuff the light, crawl back into bed. His breath falls hot and steady on my back.

I guess if you thought you had face to save you'd do it to save face. But if that's the case then I cannot imagine why Henryk bothered, and I lie in the dark for a long time fighting sleep thinking about it, and trying not to itch my eyebrow. If he just ran away, he would not care that his name went up under *Missing* on the board. Not Henryk, not in a million years.

And yet. He understands more than anyone else — more than me, too — that the world will not get better on its own. That it was not fucked up on its own, and it cannot now heal on its own. Not the world around us (which does not care if we are in it) but the one in which we live, in which we partic-ipate. The one that has a pulse. He understands that.

And at last I do understand why he did it, and I find I am the shamed one. The timing of the "arrival" of that letter: not a coincidence. I still feel that I am leaving my mother for an airy-fairy dream, just as she said, just as she feared, just as I fear. Just as Hen fears, too, and will never tell me. But what if the only way out was just wide enough for you, and no one else? What if you promised to come back and knew it wasn't a promise you could keep? To anyone, for all time. What if you left and discovered that you didn't *want* to come back? What if the bone had to break? If love does not pin you down, if love is not heavy enough to keep you in place, what on earth could be? If love is not enough then guilt cannot be enough, duty cannot be enough. But what do they weigh? What is the heaviest, what could weigh you down?

Maybe it doesn't matter. I don't know. I'm weeping again, getting both tears and blood on Hen's pillow. Whatever a cloud is, whatever it weighs, no matter how big it is, *something* moves them around: they move, they do not resist it. Nothing is so heavy that it doesn't. Look at the planet. Still moving. And still moving back to the same place it came to every year. We cannot affect that. Not with all the will in the world.

Henryk puts a knuckle in my back, as if knocking to be let in. "Are you okay?"

"Mm. Just thinking."

"What about?"

You, you, you. Only you, always you. How I thought we were going to do it, and what a disaster that would have been, and whether I wanted it or not, and I still don't know the answer. You, who I will leave, who is leaving me. "The future."

"The future?"

I shrug, and wipe my face: smell of rust. "Maybe everybody will have Cad. And everybody will be safe. Sick, and safe."

"The other option is that everyone stops having kids at all. No more Cad."

"I don't think it'll let people do that."

"Maybe." He yawns. It is academic to him. I am briefly, furiously envious. "Sleep."

"*You* sleep."

When Henryk's little wind-up clock blares, I return home, woozy with exhaustion, a little too defiant, waiting for Mom to accuse me of abandoning her to fuck Henryk so that I can shout that I didn't, but she doesn't. For a second I wonder if she realized I didn't storm back in after I stormed out, but dismiss that as too good to be true. We're all crammed in here so tightly that you pretty much always know where someone is. Recognize the breath on the far side of the wall. She looks unslept, irritated, but not actually angry. I guess it's true what they say: sleep on your anger, and it may not waken.

Tightly, she says, "Let me look at your cut."

I walk to her and hold my breath as she takes my face in her hands. One of us has to be the bigger person, I think. Her, because she's the grownup. Me, because I see how she does it. All right. All right. This is survivable. The worst is over. Now we can talk rationally.

"You must have picked at it in your sleep."

"I think so. It was bleeding a little."

"Did you put pressure on it?"

"Yes. A few minutes."

Her next questions should be "Where were you?" and "With who?" but she tightens her lips and says, "Let's go get breakfast."

We dress and head to the stairs, and I precede her in the trickle of people ahead of us. "You'll have to start thinking about storage for all that meat," I say, and turn, and she is silhouetted for a moment, and I know, *know*, a tremendous flash of knowledge, a cymbal-clash, the Annunciation in old paintings, what she is about to do, and that she will succeed.

Nothing will be taken from me, she seems to say, or the disease says, though perhaps (in the second that elapses between when I turn and when she begins her flight down the concrete steps) they are working as one; nothing will leave me, I will leave rather than be left, I have had enough of being left —

— and in the last moment, I who have never prayed, who takes everything in vain because it is what the other kids did, find myself praying to a disease. Help me! I can't do this alone!

Something responds.

In the years to come I will never know what. I throw myself up the steps as she comes down, and catch her, taking her full weight — meagre, bones in the crackling dress, screams around us — before she hits the landing, and the nameless one arranges my body in midair to curl and roll, thudding down the last few steps till we are on the flat concrete pad, and neighbours are pulling us apart, wailing in fear, and someone picks me up, and someone picks her up, and I meet her eyes: No, I try to tell her. I thought we could all be separated, but we cannot. I, and my monster, will go. You, and your monster, will stay. This is how I know I'm going.

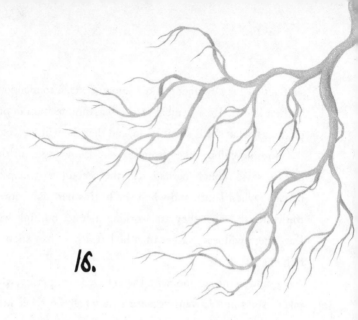

16.

The worst was over, and then it wasn't, and now something else begins. Unofficially, she is confined to our office for a week while Dr. Chan comes and chats with her. I don't know if this is therapy (which I've read about, but not actually seen). Mom sticks to her story: She didn't jump. She slipped.

"A dozen witnesses have suggested otherwise, Claire." Dr. Chan is soft-voiced, wears her hair loose over her shoulders, dark and sleek as the pelt of a black cat. Her skin has no writing on it. She knows things about minds, but I worry that she doesn't know things about the parasite. It is something you cannot know from a book.

"I happen to think," Mom says, glancing at me in the doorway, "that it's not very good for people's mental health to be accused of lying."

"No, you're right. It's not. But it's also not very good for people to lie to themselves."

"I suppose it wouldn't be."

She did jump, I tell Dr. Chan later on, a few floors down, while Yash and Mal take up self-appointed, and not very surreptitious, sentry duty. She didn't slip or tumble. She leapt, like a fleeing deer, and with the same strength and speed: I did not think I would catch her.

"It's the disease," I tell her. "I know it was. I could have lifted a car."

"Reid, that doesn't fit very well with what we know about *Cadastrulamyces*," Dr. Chan says. "The presence of the infection seems to be correlated with *fewer* occurrences of risk-taking behaviour."

"No. Believe me, okay? Trust me. I live with it. I've felt it inside: like a hand, holding your bones, pushing you around. I've felt it respond to things you'd never believe. What it does is a calculation. It does a — what do you call it. A cost-benefit analysis. There are risks, but then there are bigger risks. If the options don't look good sometimes it'll do nothing. But sometimes it'll decide between bad and worse."

"That sounds like a lot of agency for a fungal infection."

"It sounds fucking bonkers. I know. But if you thought there might be two outcomes, and all you had to work with was a body: you think — If I die, I'll never see her go. If I live, I'll be so hurt she'll have to stay. Either way it wins. It —"

"Reid. Please don't —"

"— it wins, okay? It thinks in terms of winning and losing. I know it does. It knows the best way only to keep the host body alive, or to end it, and Mom went along with it. Because it made sense to her. I don't know how I can leave her in this state. How can I?"

Dr. Chan regards me with something like astonishment. I try to review my last handful of sentences in my head, and okay, admittedly: Not good. Not real good.

"My own infection let me save her. Let me save *hers* too," I say after a minute. "I couldn't have done it myself."

"Reid."

"Don't put this down in the record, okay? Please don't." I get up unsteadily, and head to the door. "I have to go, I'm sorry. I'm supposed to go to the hospital. Dr. G has to look at my foot. Infection or whatever. I'll come back."

"I'll see you when you do," she calls.

Both of us, I almost say. We are not a team now, but we are not enemies fighting a war either. I think perhaps there has been a truce. Maybe temporary. I don't know. But know that you are dealing with two, and not one.

I think, as if I am addressing a child instead of a disease: Operation Barbarossa. You don't know what that is, do you? Maybe it's best I don't tell you.

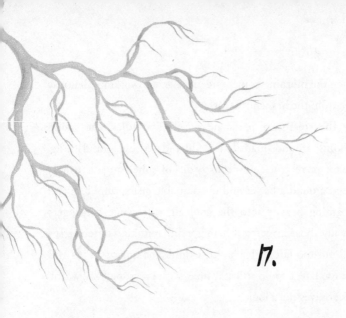

17.

Mom's week ticks down; mine does too. Boar jerky (gamey, rusty-tasting, as precious as salt) buys me a spot on a steam-cart convoy heading west on Highway 16; I will be on my own to head south after I'm dropped off, but only a short hike from the edge of the Zone. I'm worried about hiking on my busted leg, but I don't have a choice.

I know I shouldn't carry much weight, and luckily there isn't much to pack; it all fits in my woven rucksack. Clothes and hand-drawn maps, the letter, the tracker, food, water, soap, toothbrush and charcoal, my magpie painting, one book (my favourite, with the great tripartite-mouthed worm on the cover). Dr. Chan frets; Dr. Gagliardi frets; Henryk frets; Mom is serene, her final gambit, her nuclear option, failed.

Robins sing for tiny kingdoms; both sides of night are marked with their song. The ice on the river breaks up. And when the morning comes, green leaves are working their way free from the branches at last.

The steamcart parks near Sub, and idles, the sound echoing around quad. It is a dilapidated but grand thing, once a gravel truck, now mostly bits of bolted-together sheet metal around a boiler and uncountable gears, rumbling and breathing heavily into the cool air, with three passengers already aboard. Seeing it here is a different kind of terror. It's still not too late to back out, I think, looking at it. It's still not too late. I could still stay here, with everyone I know. The driver gives me a look.

"Reid."

I turn, lightheaded with terror, and see that others have joined my mother and Henryk as part of the seeing-off. McKinnon, Larsen, Koda. Aldous, impossibly, on a wheeled bed pushed by four people I don't know. Mal and Yash, smiling. Mrs. Cross. Larsen says, "Listen. This wasn't easy to find. A bunch of us had to take the damn city apart to put it together. So don't mess it up, okay?"

"What?"

"Voila," croaks Aldous, and from behind him one of the boys wheels out a bicycle — a *bicycle*, of all things. Most of the paint gone, sky-blue shreds remaining over a black frame, the wheels those weird airless ones that look like honeycombs. A bike. I thought people had busted or absconded with every single one not claimed by the Coy Scouts. My God. It's even got a basket on it. And a *bell*.

Where in the world did they find a bell? I take the handle-
bars, bracing the light frame against my hip.

"So you can get south," Larsen says, unnecessarily, "after
you get dropped off."

"Cargo's extra," the driver says.

"I'll end you where you stand."

" . . . All right, this one time."

I'm speechless, stumbling over my words. "Larsen. Koda.
All of you — how — how?! I can't take this. You need this
here. Bikes are — *how*?"

"Not easy, is how," Koda repeats, and squeezes my shoulder
with her big hand. "Go make us proud."

"I don't know how to ride a bike."

"Well, learn how, and then make us proud. Christ."

I look up into her dark eyes, trying to see a trace of pity
there — she has given me enough charity, I think, but all
I can see is determination. There is a mission, and if we
all cannot carry it out, then one of us must go and carry it
out by proxy. That, I understand. Pride is better than anger.
Better than pain. When we think we have nothing to be
proud of, we can be proud that we set a girl on her way to an
impossible dream. Yes, all right. I accept.

"I promise I'll be back," I say. No one speaks. I awkwardly
hug Henryk and push a letter into his coat pocket, and then
we stand for a moment with our hands on each other's shoulders. He's taller than me, and I don't know why I find this
strange; as strange as it is that I'm taller than Mom now. I'll

write, I want to tell him. Write to me. My address is: a dome. Instead of speaking I can only stare into his washed-out, rainy-day eyes, trying to memorize their shape and colour.

For no reason the long, amber light on his face reminds me of something we used to do when we were kids: pulling up asphalt pebbles from the road and throwing them into our tiny fires till they flared and melted. God only knew what we were breathing in, but it was always satisfying to watch them deliquesce: solid into liquid, gone like ice. I never knew why we did it. Just fun, I guess, and we were bored; but now I wonder how long ago I looked at his face in that tiny orange firelight and knew for sure that I loved him, even if he never loved me.

"I, an alligator, will return," I tell him.

Tears at last, his face wobbling. "In a wh . . . in some period, certainly, crocodile."

Yash and Mal clutch me, run their hands over my hair. I hug Mom last, a long hug, breathing in her familiar smell, resting my head on her shoulder. This at least I have never doubted. Not for any longer than a second or two, when it seemed it would be taken from me. But even that could not have succeeded in removing the love, only other things.

I had wanted to leave with one of grandma's enamel pins on my jacket, so that in some way a cycle could be unbroken — Great-grandma to Grandma to Mom to me, but I never asked for one, and of course Mom can't read my mind. She would have given me one though, I think. If she had, I would have left this boar tusk at home, secret and sharp in the bottom of my bag, wrapped in a dozen plastic bags. That's not what I want: showing up to this grand futuristic place like a caveman with a bone. A pin would have been better. A unicorn. But I did not speak. "I love you," I tell her.

"I love you."

We all shout our goodbyes and they flee for cover under a darkening dawn, the first drops of welcome rain. These days, *rain* is another word for hope. A good omen. I stow my bike, climb aboard the cart, and find a spot on a bench, pushing my bag between my legs. The driver flips up a loosely woven cover to keep out the wet, and campus disappears into darkness, except for a semicircle of light ahead and behind us, like a tunnel. I didn't say everything I meant to say, but I mean, who ever does, really. Can't be held to such an impossible standard.

As the cart turns, I get a startling glimpse of my mother's face, pale, turning back to look (no — don't look back), the trees in her cheeks seeming to surge forward to say one last farewell to the trees under my nails. One day she watched her mother die of Cad, and one day I will watch my mother die of Cad, and if I have a daughter she too will watch her mother die one day of Cad. Do they all know one another, all these different infections? Yes, they must. Mine is daughter of hers. Well, say your goodbyes: and one day we will all see each other again.

ACKNOWLEDGEMENTS

I would like to thank my agent, Michael Curry, as always, for helping to bring this novella into the world. I would also like to thank my incredibly perceptive and dedicated editor at ECW Press, Jen Albert, and our eagle-eyed copy editor, Rachel Ironstone. They shaped this into a stronger, clearer story and brought Reid and her community to life. I'm also grateful to Jessica Albert at ECW Press and Veronica Park, who created the amazing cover; I'm not sure I've ever had a cover that so beautifully and elegantly rendered the heart of a story. My local friends Jordan and Vicki Lightbown patiently answered all my questions about hunting strategies, archery, the river valley, and feral hogs (as well as supplying me with wine and endless stories!). My friend Jennifer R. Donohue probably deserves an actual medal for putting up with me during the writing, revision, and editing stages, and I am indebted to her for her humour and patience. And finally, I would like to acknowledge my long-time friends Mark McIntyre and Kim Scott, who rarely left my side when I attended the University of Alberta and without whose love, companionship, and determination I never would have graduated.

PREMEE MOHAMED is an Indo-Caribbean scientist and author based in Edmonton, Canada. She completed degrees in Biology and Environmental Conservation at the University of Alberta. She is the author of novels *Beneath the Rising* and *A Broken Darkness* and novellas *The Apple-Tree Throne, These Lifeless Things, And What Can We Offer You Tonight*, and *The Annual Migration of Clouds*. Her short fiction has appeared in a variety of print and audio venues. Upcoming work can be found at her website, premeemohamed.com.

This book is also available as a Global Certified Accessible™ (GCA) ebook. ECW Press's ebooks are screen reader friendly and are built to meet the needs of those who are unable to read standard print due to blindness, low vision, dyslexia, or a physical disability.

Purchase the print edition and receive the eBook free! Just send an email to ebook@ecwpress.com and include:

- the book title
- the name of the store where you purchased it
- your receipt number
- your preference of file type: PDF or ePub

A real person will respond to your email with your eBook attached. And thanks for supporting an independently owned Canadian publisher with your purchase!

Printed on Rolland Enviro.
This paper contains 100% post-consumer fiber,
is manufactured using renewable energy - Biogas
and processed chlorine free.

100%

PCF

PERMANENT